"AN ENTERTAINING DEBUT . . . Meet Quentin Jacoby, down-to-earth detective and a welcome new face among amateur sleuths."
—*Washington Post*

"GUT-WRENCHING AND ABSORBING!"
—*Chicago Sun-Times*

"EXCELLENT! An effective murder story that introduces an enjoyable new detective . . . New York locations add character to this very good, well-written effort."
—*Dallas Morning News*

"INTRIGUING, ENTERTAINING . . . Well-paced, tightly constructed, and not without some light touches . . . Best of all, Smith has created a potentially very popular character in the person of Quentin Jacoby."
—*Bestsellers*

"THE MURDER MYSTERY IS ALIVE AND WELL! Quentin Jacoby is attractive and unusual enough for us to want to meet him again . . . I'm hungry for Jacoby's second case."
—*Nashville Tennessean*

Great Reading from SIGNET

SIGNET MYSTERY

Jacoby's First Case

J.C.S. Smith

A SIGNET BOOK

NEW AMERICAN LIBRARY

PUBLISHED BY
THE NEW AMERICAN LIBRARY
OF CANADA LIMITED

PUBLISHER'S NOTE

This novel is a work of fiction. Names, characters, places and incidents either are the product of the author's imagination or are used fictitiously, and any resemblance to actual persons, living or dead, events, or locales is entirely coincidental.

NAL BOOKS ARE AVAILABLE AT QUANTITY DISCOUNTS WHEN USED TO PROMOTE PRODUCTS OR SERVICES. FOR INFORMATION PLEASE WRITE TO PREMIUM MARKETING DIVISION, NEW AMERICAN LIBRARY, 1633 BROADWAY, NEW YORK, NEW YORK 10019

This is an authorized reprint of a hardcover edition published by Atheneum Publishers, Inc. The hardcover edition was published simultaneously in Canada by McClelland and Stewart Ltd.

First Signet Printing, March, 1985

2 3 4 5 6 7 8 9

Ⓢ SIGNET TRADEMARK REG. U.S. PAT. OFF. AND FOREIGN COUNTRIES
REGISTERED TRADEMARK — MARCA REGISTRADA
HECHO EN WINNIPEG, CANADA

SIGNET, SIGNET CLASSIC, MENTOR, PLUME, MERIDIAN and NAL BOOKS are published in Canada by The New American Library of Canada, Limited, Scarborough, Ontario.

PRINTED IN CANADA

COVER PRINTED IN U.S.A.

Chapter 1

When the Mount Vernon Raceway opened in 1898 it was called Knickerbocker Park, and they touted it as a most gentlemanly place to watch the art of harness racing. I looked it up once at the public library. I like to know the background of the organizations I support.

The track still looks pretty good. The grass is kept up, and if the clubhouse needs paint, it doesn't show at night under the lights. When the trotters are going and the crowd is excited and the silks are bright, you can forget all about the highway and the city right outside; it's that nice. The gentry doesn't gather much for the Daily Double any more, though. There were a lot of other people lining up Monday night for the early bus back downtown.

I was getting out my exact change when I saw her. My mind was on the thirty bucks I had just contributed to the future upkeep of harness racing in New York, but it's hard to overlook a girl walking barefoot across a highway at nine o'clock at night. Cursing my luck for having the conscience of a public servant, I got out of line and walked over to the cyclone fence that separates the parking lot from the Bronx River Parkway.

"Hey, sweetheart," I yelled. "You'll live longer if you find another way of getting where you're going."

She looked in my direction, but right through me. Then she walked slowly back to the grassy bank on the side of the access road. Twenty, maybe, and thin in that way sandy blondes often are. Too thin to be really pretty. And too pale. She was dangling a pair of green sandals from her left hand, like she had started to put them on and then forgot about it. I made motions for her to wait while I circled the fence.

"Come on, sweetheart," I coaxed. "Let's see if we can find where you belong." Her pink cotton dress wasn't heavy enough for the second week in April, and her arm was bare and cold where I took it to guide her further back from the road. The highway lights showed her eyes dilated in a way I knew too well. Where she belonged was the station house, but that wasn't my business anymore.

I was beginning to think she hadn't noticed me at all, but then she finally opened her mouth.

"The Raceway Motel is just off the next exit. Fifty dollars regular, one-twenty for anything fancy. In advance. Anything."

The girl wasn't bad, but the setup stank. She made her pitch like it was a recorded message, without even bothering to look my way. I put on the grandpa act, the one I used for lost kids on the subway when I was still with the mole force.

"Not that I don't appreciate the offer," I said, "but why don't you save it for some guy your own age? My neighbor Mrs. Farbelstein would not approve, and my late wife, who put up with me for thirty years, would be hurt. So now that we've established I'm a nice old man, where can I take you where you won't go wandering across any highways?"

I had some trouble saying this. Fifty-five is not so old, and I wasn't feeling so nice, either. But that low I hadn't gotten. Besides, I wanted to see what she'd say. If she was a pro, which I doubted, she'd smell me for a cop and run like hell.

But she didn't. She didn't even move. She took the turndown so calm I almost felt insulted. I'm not that far over the hill.

"Tired," she said, to no one in particular. "Going back."

Anyway, I was right about her being new at the game. A hooker with any sense of the trade would have already by now told me just what she thought of me and split for another john.

We both stood looking out over the traffic. Three lanes north, three lanes south. Not many cars turning off for the track this time of night. She fumbled in her bag for a while, then finally

pulled out a pack of cigarettes. Benson & Hedges.
Very classy. The cigarettes and the bag they
came out of were the only substantial things
about her. It was a huge sack of some kind of
purple stuff, suede I think, with wooden beads
hanging from the ends of the fringes. I helped her
connect with a match, then grabbed her arm
again as she started walking shakily toward the
littered cross-street that leads around the Raceway and reconnects with the city. I had already
missed my bus, so what the hell.

"It's there. The next block. Across from
Louie's."

We had been walking in silence, and now each
of her words came out real slow, like it was an
effort to finish the sentence.

I stopped in front of Louie's Whamburger
Wagon, but she just kept on going across the
street, like she had already forgotten I was there.
She was concentrating on getting home before
she crashed.

She stumbled a little on the steps, but finally
found the key and vanished into the south half of
one of those two-family stucco jobs they built a
lot of in the thirties. Siamese-twin houses with a
shared wall down the middle. I hoped for her sake
she found a little something inside to pick her up.

It was funny, though. Even with the dope, and
the job that went with it, there was something
almost wholesome about her, something that
made me think she didn't really belong in that

house, in that racket. Underneath the makeup she looked like an ad for soap.

I decided to have a late supper while I considered why I hadn't turned her over to the boys. It would ruin my evening schedule, but I didn't think my date would mind. The eleven o'clock news team is very understanding.

Halfway through my whamburger I saw the kid watching me. A very ordinary kid, maybe a little better off than you'd expect in this neighborhood, his blue jeans hanging low on a body that hadn't had time to catch up with his bones. His brown hair looked like it had been through shock treatment, but he had a kind of hesitant expression I liked. I'd seen him standing by the door when I came in, but I hadn't realized he was waiting for me. As soon as he saw I had noticed him, he came over.

"Excuse me, sir. I know we haven't met, but could I talk to you for a minute? It's very important."

I waved grandly at the stool next to me, and he perched on the edge of it, shifting his legs this way and that while he tried to figure out where they would fit. He acted like a gawky kid, but close up I could see he was old enough to need a shave. His beard was coming in red.

"I've been looking for Cissy for a couple of months now, since she left home," he blurted. "I just found her two days ago. I'm sort of not sure I should bother her any more, but I saw you walk up with her, so I thought maybe . . . is she in okay shape? Do you think it would be a good idea to go over there?" He stopped as suddenly as he had started.

"That's her name?" I asked. "Sissy? Used to be an insult, not a name. But I guess times change." I was belching a little from the crummy relish they gave you in these joints.

"Cecilia." He stopped even shorter this time, banging his knees on the counter as he turned on his stool. "I, er, thought you knew her. My mistake." He was trying to make his embarrassment sound like toughness. It was like a cocker spaniel playing mastiff. I threw him a doggie biscuit for trying.

"I know her enough to say she's in rotten shape. But go see for yourself. She won't mind."

The kid vanished and was back in time for my second cup of coffee. Which was not long, when you consider how little they put in those little plastic cones.

"She just opened the door and stood there. Very polite, like I was the Fuller Brush man, or invisible or something. Then she shut the door in my face."

"Have a seat," I said, and went through the waving routine again. The kid sat down and automatically reached for a napkin. Then he said the first logical thing I'd heard that evening.

"If you're not a friend of Cissy's, who are you? Are you with the police or something?"

"Quentin Jacoby," I announced grandly. "Former sergeant, New York City Transit Police. Now retired. Current residence, Co-op City. Current occupation, zilch."

I thought about being a subway cop. There's a whole world down there, and I used to live in it. The city beneath the city. You can get a haircut, eat a hot dog, have your shoes fixed, all underground. Three and a half million people come through every day. But after a while you don't even see the ordinary people. The only ones you notice are the purse-snatchers, the muggers, the rapists, the hop-head kids working their way to immortality with a can of spray paint. Or maybe they're the normal ones. I don't remember. I retired early, to spend more time with Bea when she got sick. No good thinking about that. Back to the present. The kid just sat there, shredding his napkin into little pieces, so I kept on talking.

"Like I said, retired. You can retire real young if you work for the city. So now I'm enjoying my so-called golden years. Sometimes I go to the pistol range at the Police Academy to work out. I read a little. I play a little poker, watch the tube. Mostly I go to the track. Apart from my neighbor's kids and your friend with the funny name, you're the first person under fifty I've talked to this month. So please don't tell me now you're an agent for a nice widow lady who would really know how to make me a home."

I don't usually shoot off to strangers, listening

being my specialty, but I got a kick out of reviewing my exciting jet-set life. I waited for some reaction, but he just sat there pushing the little pieces of paper around the counter with his index finger. I took another breath.

"So that's who I am. Who are you, kid? And what started you thinking about the police? You want a cop?"

He woke up at that.

"I don't want a cop! I don't want any more police ever." Then he went on more slowly. "But my family doesn't want me to have anything more to do with her, Cissy's parents are worthless, and the Social Aid people she'd been seeing won't even talk to me. I need help."

He gave me a long, earnest look, like he was expecting me to sign on right there.

"That still doesn't tell me much," I pointed out. "Got a name?"

He blushed, half stood up, and held out his hand across the relish pots.

"I'm sorry. My name is Peter Hecht. I live over in Larchmont, near the Sound. I go to Edgewater Day School there. So does Cissy, or at least she did, and I can't just let her slip off like this, even if . . ."

A nice kid, I thought, but possibly a little slow. He seemed to have just considered that maybe I wasn't the help he wanted. I waited a while, but nothing came.

"Even if what?"

He blushed again. He was good at blushing. I wanted to shake him for being so clean and so dumb.

"I'm sorry," he apologized again. "Just forget it. I'm kind of upset, and I guess I make things seem bigger than they are. Anyway, don't worry about my ravings. It's nice to have met you, but I have to go now."

He looked worried as he slid away from the counter, but I wasn't about to stop him. I have always held that there is no point in butting into someone's life when he doesn't want it butted into. If Peter Hecht wanted to fade, that was his business. Let him take his troubles back to the well-cushioned solace of Larchmont. When I was riding the subway, I got used to unfinished stories that were cut off by a pair of sliding doors. Usually the ending I made up was better than anything that could happen, anyway. This time it wasn't, but I didn't find that out for another few days.

By that time the girl was dead.

Chapter 2

The phone started to ring the next afternoon as I was coming down the hall with my laundry. I dropped the basket outside the door, hoping no one would steal the towels, and caught the phone on what sounded like the last ring.

"Is this Mr. Quentin Jacoby, who used to be a transit policeman?"

My first thought was that "This Is Your Life" had hit the bottom of the barrel. My second thought was of the kid. This time I was right.

"Mr. Jacoby? This is Peter Hecht. From the hamburger place last night?" His voice went up at the end of each sentence, like he wasn't really sure who he was or where he'd been. I grunted a sort of recognition.

"Ah huh."

"First, Mr. Jacoby, I'd like to apologize for the way I walked off last night. I was in kind of a daze, and I really had to get my head together. I'm sorry."

"It's okay, kid. But don't tell me you hunted me out of the sixty-four Jacobys in Co-op City to tell me you're sorry."

"Sixty-five," he corrected me. His voice got stronger, with a snap of pride. "But only one whose name begins with Q."

I turned to see if my towels were still by the open doorway. So far, so good.

"I called because I need someone to work with me, someone who knows what Cissy looks like. I can pay you for your time." His voice got very adult here, then lapsed back into adolescence as the imitation wore off. "You did . . . well, you did say you hadn't much to do."

The kid wasn't making too much sense, or maybe it was the fabric softener I'd been inhaling. I listened to him breathe for a while, then took over my end of the conversation.

"Look, Mr. Peter Hecht," I spelled out as patiently as I could, "I don't know you from a hole in the wall. Maybe that wouldn't keep me from helping you out, but I also don't know what it is you want. You wanted to find your girl. Well, you found her. Maybe she wasn't exactly the same girl you lost. Unfortunately, I am not Dear Abby to reunite young lovers, nor am I about to start a stakeout in a hamburger stand so I can watch every john she brings in. If you ask me, that girl is supporting a habit, which maybe makes this a case for the police. Which, as I told you last night, I'm not."

The kid's voice held, but I could imagine him blushing.

"I'm sorry I didn't come to the point," he said tensely. "Cissy's missing again, this time from that house in Mount Vernon. I went back there this morning. The woman who answered the bell says she never heard of Cissy, or anyone like her, and slammed the door in my face. I watched Cissy there for three days, and you saw her, too." His voice had risen to almost a shout. "Something's wrong, Mr. Jacoby," he insisted. Then his voice got softer. "I'd like you to help me find her."

So this is how, at the age of fifty-five, I entered my new career as an unlicensed private detective. It wasn't exactly like in the movies. Instead of a gun in my pocket, I had yesterday's racing form, and instead of a gorgeous blonde, my client was a high school senior who seemed a little young for his age. He was going to pay me, I suppose, out of his allowance.

The whole thing sounded like a put-on, but there was something in his voice that said he wasn't kidding. I am not a sentimental guy, but I don't like to leave a person who's frightened and lost. And besides, he was right—I was bored. I told him to pick me up in an hour and went out to retrieve my laundry.

Chapter 3

Co-op City is another of New York's attempts at the utopian housing project, a high-rise metropolis with its own stores, schools, and parks: the city of the future, built on landfill over the bones of a dead amusement park. The idea was to mix inexpensive co-ops and convenient services to create the sense of community that was falling apart in most other places.

Maybe it does that for some people. Me, I feel like the real community is on the other side across the moat of highways that separates us from the rest of the world. Here it seems like it's mostly a lot of old people playing bridge and making ashtrays at the Leisure Center, killing time until time kills them. But the rates are good and the rooms are bright, and after Bea couldn't manage stairs any more it seemed like we didn't have much choice. It's still an okay place to live, probably better than most, and safer. But every time I leave I feel like I'm being sprung.

Which maybe explains why I was standing

outside fifteen minutes early, watching the start of the afternoon commuter pile-up on the New England Thruway. I was looking for the late-model white Chevy Caprice that the kid had told me was "sort of" his. After about five minutes I saw him turn off the Thruway and onto the access road that leads to my building. I waved him over to a hydrant before he got lost forever trying to find a parking space. He cut the engine as I opened the door.

As soon as I wedged myself into the bucket seat he held out a fifty-dollar bill. I stared at it. Suddenly the whole thing seemed like an embarrassing joke.

"I meant it about paying you," he said. "I want you to know I'm serious. Because we don't have much time."

"What do you mean?"

He handed me the afternoon *Post*, open to one of the inside pages. "I saw this just after I talked to you," he said. His finger nearly poked a hole in the paper as he pointed to a story on the top of the page, just above a big ad for hospital insurance for senior citizens.

SECOND BRUTAL SLAYING IN MOUNT VERNON

Unidentified Victim Found at Curb

Police are investigating the murder of an unidentified young woman whose body was found in a green plastic garbage bag early this morning outside 2933 Eurydice Avenue, Mount Vernon. The victim was apparently stabbed to death and had been dead since approximately midnight, according to a police spokesman.

The body, that of an olive-skinned brunette in her late teens, had been badly mutilated but not sexually assaulted. No identification of any kind was found on the body.

No connection has been established to the brutal murder two days ago of Rochelle Bellini, 20, whose body was found under similar circumstances two blocks from that of the latest victim.

Police said . . .

Olive-skinned brunette. At least it wasn't the kid's girlfriend. The story went on to say how the body apparently had been taken from someplace else and dumped on the street sometime around 3 A.M., where it had sat until the sanitation men had found it in the morning. None of the locals knew from nothing, but there was plenty of squawking about the need for more police protection. The woman who lived at 2933 Eurydice Avenue was hysterical and kept on yelling she was next.

A typical slice of urban life. I remembered another couple of murders like this around Christ-

mas time. Everyone got all steamed up for a week
or two, with lots of hype from the news people,
and then the whole thing blew over. They never
even caught anyone. I skimmed the page again,
looking for something I had missed.

"So?" I asked finally.

"Twenty-nine thirty-three," Hecht repeated.
"That's the house Cissy was in. That's where you
took her last night." We weren't going anywhere,
but his hands gripped the steering wheel. "I went
there this morning, Mr. Jacoby, and the woman
who answered the door said she'd never heard of
Cissy. She said she'd call the police if I bothered
her again. Two murders, Mr. Jacoby. What if
Cissy is next?" His voice was rising toward panic.
I cut him off.

"Calm down, kid," I said, though I didn't feel
very calm myself. I was used to petty thefts and
shake-downs on the crosstown local, but sadistic
murders were out of my line. I left the force
before that got to be part of a day's work. I
thought about it a while, then took the fifty and
put it in my wallet.

"Let's go someplace where we can talk, kid.
You know the way to City Island?"

He didn't, which wasn't really too surprising,
but with me navigating we got there in about
fifteen minutes.

City Island, the poor man's Newport, is tied to
the Bronx by a short bridge that keeps it from
drifting off into the high-rent districts of West-

chester County. Unless you like boats or seafood or are one of the few people who actually live on the place, you'd never have any reason to go there. The marinas were just cleaning up for the spring, and the firemen and bail bondsmen who have bungalows out there hadn't begun to think about vacations.

The seafood stands were open, though. The guy at the counter cursed me out for giving him a fifty, but he made the change. I took the two plates of fish and fries and motioned Hecht to follow me out onto the pier. By June the place is jammed and you can't hear yourself think for the transistor radios, but around this time of year it's a nice quiet spot to go if you want to talk to somebody. And Peter Hecht wanted to talk to somebody.

I handed him a plate, but he hardly noticed. He just put it down beside him on the concrete.

"Cissy looks older, but she's only seventeen," he began, settling himself against the railing. "I don't know when she got on hard drugs. We used to smoke a little dope at parties, and drink some, but everybody does that. I guess she started buying, though, and met some people who got her into bigger stuff. Cocaine mostly. I don't know how she paid for it. Her parents aren't too good about remembering to give her money, and she always used to be kind of broke. You know, lots of charge accounts but no cash." I didn't know, but far be it from me to interrupt.

"Anyway," he continued, "she got in with this tough crowd about a year and a half ago and got busted once at a party in Harlem. The police weren't too bad since she was a minor, but her parents weren't exactly supportive. Cissy was in a juvenile home for almost a week because no one could get through to her family. They had gone to one of those health spas in California or Florida or someplace, but Cissy didn't know which one and the maid just walked out the back door and never came back when she saw the police.

"When her parents finally got home, they acted as though Cissy had gotten arrested to spite them. Their way of punishing her was to put her in complete isolation. Two weeks—no school, no telephone, no visitors, no going out. They wouldn't take anything away from her—that would be too cruel, they figured. Just no contact with the world. Cissy doesn't get along too well with her stepfather, and she made a big deal of not opening her mouth for the whole time, since she decided total obedience would really bug him. Like, she'd answer the telephone and just stand there, not saying anything. She wouldn't talk to the new maid, or the gardener, or anyone."

It sounded like a real happy group. I myself grew up in a big family, with lots of noise and yelling. Since Bea died, I can't get used to the quiet.

"So where do you fit in?" I asked. I watched

the gulls circle closer as they smelled out food.

"That's when we got to be friends," Peter explained. "It was almost a year ago. I used to see her outside all the time. She would sit on the lawn, reading or just looking at the sky. One time, I remember seeing her cut her hair. She just took a scissors and cut off about two inches, without even looking. There was hair all over the grass. She wouldn't talk to me, but we had a kind of game of waving.

"Then, one day, she wasn't there. I went up on the lawn and started looking for her. I poked around the garden and even went behind the garage—I'm surprised the maid didn't take me for a prowler and call the police. Suddenly I heard a rattle and there she was, up in an apple tree, just about hidden in apple blossoms. She had a radio going, tuned to one of those talk shows.

"We started going out after her quarantine was over, but then about six months ago Cissy started back on dope again. I didn't even know for a while, except that she sometimes sounded really strange on the phone. Then one day I saw her with this real dude of a black guy, and she didn't even recognize me, she was so far gone." His voice took on a new irony. "You might say I was a little bitter."

I don't think he'd ever talked to anyone about her before. It was like he was getting it straight in his own mind. I could tell there was a lot more to his story, but the sun was setting and it was getting cold on the pier, so I suggested we move on to the track and catch the early races.

"I'm listening," I assured him, "but I've also got to do some thinking, and I like to keep moving for that. Besides, Frank the parking lot attendant is a friend of mine, and I want to see the look on his face when I arrive in style with my new chauffeur. And," I added conclusively, "if we want to find this Cissy of yours, it's time we moved in a little closer to where we last saw her."

We left the gulls squawking over Hecht's abandoned fries.

Chapter 4

I have always favored the Mount Vernon Raceway over Belmont or Aqueduct or any of the other New York tracks, for two reasons.

First, Mount Vernon features harness racing, standardbred horses and a driver in a sulky, and harness racing is the working man's sport. You don't find any Vanderbilts hanging around the paddocks at Mount Vernon—your typical owner here is three dry cleaners who have gone in on shares on a single nag.

Second, the way you get into the grandstand is the way you get into the subway—you buy a token and go through the turnstile. Call it a trainman's holiday, but it gives a certain continuity to my life.

The track was just opening when we bought our tokens that night, but they were already announcing the fifth race by the time the kid wound up his story. We'd been sitting in the grandstand all that time, but they might have been running zebras for all I got to see of the action.

What it all boiled down to was that this girl had stopped being his girl. She was flunking out of school, getting in with junkies and dealers, and then, like they always do, she ran away. Not that her parents tried to stop her, from what I gathered. It was a pretty standard story, but I guess it was new to Hecht. Still, there were some funny things about the history of Miss Cissy Holder, and I started pacing down the stairs of the grandstand as I tried to figure them out.

The kid was right behind me, and I turned around more than once, trying to figure how he had gotten hooked in with a girl like that—one who had trouble like a black star on her forehead. It had to be more than a high school romance, even if they were more advanced than kids were when I was in school. But every time I looked around all I saw was a nice, clean kid picking his way down the unfamiliar tiers. A kid with a thing for skinny girls with sandy blonde hair.

And then again, why Mount Vernon? Granted, maybe a girl from around New York wouldn't be as much of a hick as a runaway from Kansas City or Schenectady, the kind who has a fight with her parents and then heads off for a dream mecca spelled Greenwich Village. Granted she even knew enough to stay away from the main strips where the police call to round up the people out on the street supporting a habit. Still, Mount

Vernon is not a city you just drift to and get an apartment in a lower-middle-class neighborhood. There was some connection I had missed.

We were down by the betting windows on the lower level when the kid grabbed my arm.

"There she is!" He was pointing at one of those closed-circuit televisions they have all around for people who don't like to mix their gambling with fresh air. All I saw, though, was a plumpish, too-bright blonde who had once been a looker but who was fading fast as she got near the wrong side of forty. She was standing in front of the screen, having an argument with a well-dressed older man. I checked the television screen itself to make sure, but the girl wasn't there either. Not unless she was riding a sulky.

"That's the woman, Mr. Jacoby!" Hecht said loudly. "The one at the house who said she'd never heard of Cissy." He paused, staring. "But the man with her is Dr. Ward." His voice trailed off in confusion. I grabbed his collar and jerked him back around the corner.

"Are you making me out for some kind of patsy," I snapped, "standing there pointing like the star witness on Perry Mason? Because I'm bigger than you are, and stronger, and if you've got any plans for getting me into dirty business, I'll break your neck."

The kid's eyes were wide and glassy and he looked just about ready to faint from fear. I calmed down a little and got my voice under control. Somehow it made me furious that after all those hours of listening I still didn't know what the kid was talking about. Lucky the crowd was so loud no one else heard me.

"Now listen to me," I said. "If your girl really is in trouble, then this isn't a game we're playing. So who is this Dr. Ward? And who else don't I know about? What's going on that you're holding out from me? If you're serious about finding this girl, you've got to level with me and stop acting like this is some kind of a scavenger hunt we're on."

"There's nothing to tell you," Peter gulped. "I've told you everything that matters. Really. I mean, I don't think Dr. Ward can have anything to do with this. I just don't understand what he's doing here with that woman."

I still had my hands on his collar, and I guess maybe I shook him a little, just to keep him going. Anyway, he took a deep breath, like he was going to recite in class.

"Dr. Ward lives in Larchmont, not far from my parents, but that's not how I know him. He takes private patients and also teaches at the hospital in that shopping center, I think . . . you know, the one we passed just before we turned off for the Raceway? Anyway, the main thing I know is, he gives these talks all the time, at schools and the Y and like that, about birth control and drug abuse and VD and that kind of stuff. Everybody likes him, and a lot of people go to see him just to talk.

I went to dancing school with his son when we were about ten," he added, "but I haven't seen him for a long time. I wonder—"

"Did Cissy Holder ever go to talk to this guy Ward?" I interrupted.

Peter's face brightened. "Oh, yeah! Maybe that's it. Maybe he's been helping her, and that's how he knows that woman. He had people come around to his house a lot on Sundays, and Cissy used to go. It was part of the deal with the juvenile court, after she got arrested that time." He started to move off. "I'll go ask Dr. Ward if he knows where Cissy is."

The kid needed to be on a leash, he was that dumb.

"And get your girl in real trouble?" I said, stopping him before he had really started to move. "Because if she isn't there already, a stupid question could do it. Don't you think that woman is going to remember you for the kid who was nosing around this morning? And didn't she tell you she'd never heard of Cissy Holder? If you ask me, the lady's running a business out of that house on Eurydice Avenue, and if your friend the doctor is the great muck-a-muck you say he is, he isn't going to like your making the connection between them. If there is a connection. And if there isn't, it's still not going to do you any good telling the world that you're out playing junior detective."

I sounded tough, but in a way I liked the kid's

lack of smarts—it made me feel like I knew what I was doing. I checked around the corner. The two of them were still standing there in front of the TV screen, both of them furious but keeping it low. You could tell it wasn't the first time they'd had a fight. I turned back to Peter.

"A while ago you shelled out fifty bucks for someone who knew his way around, so now let me do the steering. We're going to wait right here until those two break up. Then we're going to walk out, real casual, and just happen to meet this Dr. Ward. I'm your Uncle Quentin from Miami, the black sheep of the family, and I'm making you show me the sights. You might just mention that you haven't seen Cissy for a while. You know, casual, like you're making conversation. Can you do it?"

His voice went through one of those changes I was getting used to, from all boy to all man. "I can do it," he answered.

I checked around the corner again.

"Then let's go."

Without his lady friend, the doctor was pure class. Tall and solid, with lots of that thick gray hair that inspires confidence. He held himself like he knew he was three cuts above the riffraff that hangs around under the stands. You could tell he'd have a good bedside manner, the kind that makes a lot of female patients feel sick in the small hours of the morning. Only his face didn't match. It was the color of old borscht, and it clashed badly with his brown tweed jacket. He made a good show when he saw us coming, though, and stretched out his hand to the kid.

"Why, hello, Peter. What brings you here? Come to watch my horse in the last race? I didn't know you were a fan of the trotters." His voice matched his hair. They both made you want to trust him. I resisted the impulse.

Peter shook hands, a little nervous but very polite. "Hello, Dr. Ward. I'd like you to meet Mr. —that is, my Uncle Quentin. I'm showing him around this week, since I'm on vacation. He's, uh, interested in horses."

I shot out my hand before Ward could begin fumbling for a last name.

"Always happy to meet someone else who follows the trotters," I said, smiling like an idiot. I rummaged through my mind, trying to think of a classy phrase to go with being a Hecht relative. "Someone who still appreciates the noble art of driving," I managed to get out. "If you'll tell us your horse, we'll be glad to back her. We were just going to place a little bet." The last part at least was true. I figured I might as well invest some of the dough the kid had given me.

"That's very kind of you," Ward said absently. Then he straightened his tweed shoulders and gave me a cordial smile. "Doctor's Dilemma is the lady's name. She's a pacer, actually—I like a fast race, and the pacers do have it over the trotters on that. This is only her second race this season and I can't promise you anything, but her trainer is hoping for the best." He smiled again, like a blessing, then turned back to Peter with a kind of friendly severity.

"I haven't seen you in quite a while, my good man. Have you abandoned us on Sundays?"

The kid's voice was hollow, but steady. It was his big change. "I haven't been seeing much of Cissy Holder lately," he croaked. "I guess I was just used to coming with her. Do you know where she is?" My hand tightened on his arm, but Ward's answer was quick and unconcerned.

"Why, at home, I assume. You know I don't force people to come to the sessions." He turned to me. "That's the whole point, isn't it? Reaching out to young people who have rebelled against pressure and regimentation. Letting them be themselves, having a place where they can talk and be comfortable and know their opinions are respected."

· I tried to nod sagely. Most of the reaching out I had done to kids had been to nab some young punk before he made off with another purse.

"Well, if you'll excuse me, I'm going to get back to the clubhouse," Ward apologized. "Usually I'm at the paddock before a race, but I guess I'm a bit skittish myself tonight."

He laughed nervously and glanced for a second back at the corner where he had left the blonde. "Glad to have met you, Mr. Hecht." He was nodding at me, and I decided that was as good a name as any, so I nodded back.

"We'll be looking for you one of these Sundays, Peter," he called cheerily as he went toward the escalator.

Peter stared at him. "He doesn't even know Cissy's gone," he said when Ward had gotten a good way off.

"Doesn't seem to," I agreed, and headed for the betting windows. I put a ten spot on the doctor's baby to place. No sense going overboard on a tip from a stranger. Sure enough, she came in fourth, nosed out by Junior Miss. Nothing in the last two races looked promising. I checked my watch and decided there was still time to visit the suburbs.

Chapter 5

"I thought we were going to Eurydice Avenue," Peter protested when I told him to head north from the Raceway.

"Nope," I answered. "I think we'll stay clear of there just now. I don't imagine the police like having two unexplained murders in three days, and I bet they've got the area pretty well covered. Besides," I added, "I don't know as you want to make yourself too conspicuous over there. A strange guy at eleven o'clock at night ringing the bell at the house where they just found a body, saying he wants to see some other girl—not everybody might take it the right way. You know what I mean?"

"Yeah," he agreed glumly. "I know what you mean." He paused a moment. "The world sure is a sewer." He paused again. "Where *are* we going?"

At forty miles an hour, it was about time he asked.

"We are not going anywhere, at least not for

long. You are going to take me to Larchmont, and
you're going to show me where Cissy lives, and
where Dr. Ward lives. Then you're going to drop
me off at Co-op City. And then you are going
home. Got that? No hiding in the bushes. No
cruising around the block waiting to see if you
can catch a glimpse. Home. I assume you have
parents, and they probably expect to see you
around from time to time." From what he'd been
telling me about family life in the gilded suburbs
I wasn't so sure about that last part, but it
seemed like a good guess.

"My parents don't have anything to do with
this," Peter retorted. "They're nice people—don't
think they aren't. It's just that . . . well, I'm the
youngest, and they think I'm still a baby. They
made me promise I'd stop seeing Cissy, and it
would really get them if they thought I was lying.
They think I'm in the city at a party with some
friends from school." He looked at me right in the
face for a second, then turned back to the traffic.
"Please don't get in touch with them."

"I've got to let them know if there's any
trouble," I said. "After all, they're paying me,
aren't they? Even if they don't know it?" I
expected that to hit a sore point, but the kid
answered me right back.

"No, they're not. I got that money from the
bank this morning, and I'll have another fifty
dollars for you tomorrow. I have eight hundred
dollars my grandmother left me when she died.

It's all mine, and I can't think of anything I'd rather use it for than to keep Cissy out of trouble. But if you want to quit, I'm sure I can find someone else to help me. A real detective."

The kid was right. I apologized. "Okay, I'm sorry. We're even now. But I meant it about staying home. There's nothing we can do by skulking around tonight, and I want to talk to some people tomorrow without any familiar faces around. Call me around noon, and I'll let you know what happened. If I'm not there, keep calling until you get me." If I never get back, call the morgue, I thought, but I didn't have to tell him everything. Not for just fifty dollars.

We drove for a while longer, then turned off onto a series of winding residential streets. I took a sighting on the Royal Touch Beauty Salon, and counted blocks from there. I was at four and a half when Peter pulled to the curb.

"Dr. Ward's house is that white one at the end of the road," he explained. "The one with the columns. It's a dead-end street—their backyard leads right out onto the water. They have some boats. The Sound is nice for sailing around here."

He stopped the travelogue and turned around a little in his seat. "I guess it doesn't matter," he continued, "since he doesn't know my family or anything, but are you still going to be my uncle?" The way he said it made me think I wasn't much like any other uncles he had. But that was his loss.

"I don't know, kid. I'll have to see how things go," I answered absently. I was watching the house.

A few seconds after we had pulled up, the drapes in the living room had been pulled aside. I had seen a woman in a bathrobe peer at us, and caught a glimpse of the comfortable-looking room behind her. It had made me feel queer, spying and being spied on, both. I was glad when she'd closed the curtains.

While we sat there the downstairs lights went out, and then the upstairs ones, too, a few moments later. If Mrs. Ward had been waiting up for her husband, she'd given up the watch and gone to bed. Time for us to move, too.

"Let's get to the Holder place," I said.

Peter filled me in on the family as we were driving over, back across the Post Road and six blocks past the Royal Touch in the other direction. You don't go fast at night on those narrow streets. I already knew that Cissy was an only child, that her parents had been divorced when she was about two, and that her mother had married Holder when Cissy was ten. As far as I could gather, the mother wasn't interested in much besides having a lot of money and feeling good. The Holders had been rich forever. Cissy didn't get along with her stepfather even after he adopted her, and mama tended to side with the husband. After all, he was financing all those trips and parties.

The house certainly fit the picture. It was dark stone, built to look like a castle. There were two wings off the main part of the house, and a round tower with a pointed roof stuck in the bend where the building went around a corner. You could have held a joust or something on the front lawn. The lights were still on, but there was nothing to see.

I kissed Camelot goodbye and asked Peter to drop me off at the Pelham Bay IRT station instead of taking me home. The trains run all night, and, except for rush hour, I've always found a subway car a good place to relax and think things over. That's why I used to hate being assigned to the shuttle between Grand Central Station and Times Square—no time to think anything through. Some guys like the excitement, I guess, but for me a nice dull ride out and around Pelham Bay was as good as a week on the beach in Miami.

Chapter 6

The next morning I stood in the shower and considered what I should wear for my break into society. The fact is, I hadn't put on a tie for a year and a half. The only decent jacket I own is a blue and white houndstooth I got a few weeks before Bea died. She said the hospital was boring enough without having to see me in the same old windbreaker day after day, and that she wanted to remember me as the dashing fella she knew I was.

That was the same day she started in on how I should get married again after she was gone. It depressed the hell out of me, but I took the Broadway local right down to Barney's and stood there with the longest face in the world, telling them to fix me up with something snappy in a 40 Regular. Bea was right about the windbreaker, though. As I hauled the jacket out of its cleaner's plastic, I could see her winking at me.

So there I was, all dressed up at seven-fifteen in the morning. I switched on the TV. They were doing a feature on the early-bird news on how all the stores were jammed yesterday with mothers taking their kids to buy clothes for Easter. Every school in the city was out for vacation. Right now kids were running outside with their skateboards, or lingering over their Fruit Loops, or maybe just staying late in bed. The muggers and hustlers were tasting the novelty of not playing hooky. Storekeepers, from the yarmulke-makers on Hester Street to the bodega owners on upper Broadway, were enlisting their kids as child labor to get them through the holiday rush. It looked like a swell day for finding a lost teen-ager who didn't want to be found.

Time enough for breakfast, I decided, and headed down to the donut shop, nearly breaking my neck on the auto speedway Mrs. Munoz's eight-year-old had set up in the hall outside my door. I bought a *Daily News* and looked at the pictures while I walked. The first six pages were about even on cute stories about the Easter Bunny and screaming headlines about the latest rash of murders. Gangland slaying in Hoboken. Pimp pushes tootsie off Brooklyn Bridge. Battered body washed ashore at Great Neck. At least there wasn't anything new from Eurydice Avenue.

Maybelle's Baked-While-U-Sleep-Bottomless-Coffee-Pot Donut Shop usually gets a big rush before work, around 6 A.M., and then another surge around ten when the guys on unemployment turn out. Right now the place was pretty empty.

I dropped onto a stool at the counter next to Sam Fuentes. Sam is one of the few people in my building who is not trying to marry me off, which makes him something of a pal. Before he moved here, he spent most of his sixty-seven years selling homemade sno-cones in Central Park. Every morning from April to October he'd buy a big block of ice and put it on the cart along with the bottles of his special syrups—pineapple, mango, coconut, and something which was supposed to be orange but tasted more like a cross between grapefruit and lye. If you wanted a cone, Sam would shave off a cup full of slivers from his block of ice, give it a squirt of syrup, and find himself twenty cents up in the world.

Most guys like Sam end up pushing their carts until they drop dead, but Sam was different. In 1941 he decided that his contribution to the war effort would be to get a steady job, so for the next five years he worked in a factory in Jersey. It wasn't much of a career, but it was enough to qualify him for Social Security. The minute he turned sixty-five, Sam sold his cart and moved into a two-room apartment in my building. We see each other in the lobby or at the elevator sometimes, but most of our conversations are here at Maybelle's, over the kind of rotten, non-nutritious breakfast that breaks a woman's heart. Every once in a while we get together for dinner I drag him down to the Lower East Side for some good kosher cooking, he takes me out for feasts of *arroz con pollo* and beer.

Sam is a man of considerable wisdom, part of which consists of being surprised at nothing. Still, I decided not even to try to explain my new career as a private eye. I could just hear him cackling at the idea of interrupting a comfortable retirement, with all the daytime TV I wanted, to go outside and look for a no-good dirty daughter of a whore who should be left to rot in the filth of her sins. Unless, of course, I was getting a piece of the action myself. Sam tends to talk that way. So instead I let him tell me a story about how this young chick with legs like jackhammers had been dying to set him up in style in 1956. With his accent, the key word came out more like "yak-kammers." Then we made plans to go out drinking some time soon.

This took about forty-five minutes. By then I figured it was okay to set out. It was time to see if I could retrace Cissy Holder's steps by going back to where she had started.

Chapter 7

The logical place to start was with Cissy's parents, but our meeting at the track last night had made me itchy to know more about this Dr. Ward. His answering service told me he was in his office Monday, Thursday, and Saturday, and at the hospital Tuesday and Friday. Today was Wednesday. I figured I might find him at home.

Getting to Larchmont from the Bronx without a car is not easy. Larchmont probably likes it that way. First you have to take a bus from Co-op City to the Post Road. From there you transfer to another bus for the five-mile trip down the Post Road to Larchmont, and then it's a ten-minute walk down the broad, shady residential streets with wide lawns until you hit the shoreline of the Long Island Sound. Except, of course, you never actually get that far. Between the water and the poor slobs who ride the bus is a solid wall of yacht clubs and private houses, the kind you can only get to from roads marked "Private Access—Not a Public Thoroughfare." It's not like Beverly Hills, though, where they have hired guards to show you that the signs mean business. Nobody stopped me when I walked up Pilgrim Point Road to the house Peter Hecht had pointed out the night before.

In the daylight the house looked less like an imitation of some place Washington had slept in and more like what it was, a big suburban spread built around the turn of the century, when Westchester was coming into its own as a commuter district for New York City. The white walls turned out to be cream-colored shingles, and the columns were holding up one of those wide verandas you still see on older houses. To the right of the house was a big white flagpole set in a circle of bricks, but nobody had raised the colors.

I wasn't sure how I was going to get into Ward's house, but I was saved the trouble of trying. I was halfway up the walk when the door opened and a tall, handsome woman of about forty-five came out. It was the one I'd seen at the window last night. Today her dark hair was tied in a loose bun at the back of her neck, and the pink and tan wool suit she was wearing did not come from Gimbel's basement. She stopped dead when she saw me, and started backing up so fast the young Adonis behind her stepped on her heels.

"Oh, Christ," he exclaimed. "I'm terribly sorry, Mother. Are you all right? Can I do anything?"

This must be the son Hecht had gone to danc-

ing school with. He certainly looked like the
doctor's son—well-built and well-off, with an
impressive tan for so early in the year. He was
wearing one of those cotton knit sport shirts that
come with an alligator instead of a label, and he
had a good pair of shoulders to fill it out. His
blond hair was cut short and combed into a
perfect part, his corduroy pants had a crease in
them, and his loafers were polished better than
any shoes I'd seen since I'd left the army. A real
lady-killer. Next to him, Peter Hecht looked like a
derelict.

While the two of them inspected the damage to
mama's stockings, I speculated on how many
Bloody Marys for breakfast it would take to turn
about six feet three inches of golden youth into
the beefy respectability of his father. I didn't get
far in my calculations before I was interrupted.

"Who are you?" the woman asked sharply.
"What do you want?" Her tone hinted I'd better
not take up more than twenty seconds of her
time. At least she didn't recognize me as the
Peeping Tom from outside her window.

"Well, ma'am, I was hoping you could give me
some help. Mrs. Ward?" I put it as a question,
but she didn't seem in a hurry to introduce
herself, so I went on.

"You see, it's about my niece," I said. "She
used to talk about what a great guy Dr. Ward
was, and, I, er, I was hoping I could talk to him
about her."

Dead silence. The kid stepped up to stand next to his mother, and the two of them glared at me. I started talking faster.

"Don't get me wrong. She's a good kid, but you know how things are these days and with her mother worried sick, well . . ." I trailed off before it got too ridiculous, and stuck out my hand. "Quentin Jacoby, ma'am. Is your husband at home?"

She stood there looking at my hand like I'd offered her a piece of horse flop on a paper plate. Then she turned around a bit, softening her expression to go with her tone.

"Harry, could you just get the garage door for me? You know how it sticks."

Golden boy hesitated, still glaring at me. I could see the muscles working in his jaw. Clean, lean, and nervous as hell. About what?

"Don't worry, dear," his mother said, "I really can take care of myself." She looked ten years younger as she smiled at his concern. "I'm just going to talk to this man and then I'm going shopping. I'll be right back."

"I still think I should go with you."

"Whatever for?" she laughed. "Now be an angel and get the car out for me."

She watched Harry until he was a good way down the driveway, and then she turned back to me. There was nothing angelic in the clipped, cold voice whose tone said "drop dead" as clear as you could want.

"Dr. Ward has canceled all his home appointments for the foreseeable future," she announced. "Nor is he in at the moment. Nor do I know where he can be reached. I'm sorry I can't help you with your family troubles, Mr. Jacoby, but I'm afraid I don't really care to involve myself in my husband's charitable works." Her lips tightened, and she picked angrily at her jacket. "To be frank, I don't really care about your niece. But I'm sure Eli would. In fact, I'm sure his patients are all he cares about."

She started pulling on her gloves, and shot me a bitter smile. "In a few days, I shall be leaving for Reno, Nevada, where I will lie in the sun for three weeks waiting for the privilege of not being Mrs. Eli Ward. After that you can bring all the waifs and strays you like to camp on our doorstep. Harry will be back in school then. But until he is, and until I leave, I plan to spend as much time with him as possible." Her voice grew querulous. "I owe my son that little bit of normality to look back on when he has to face the collapse of his parents' marriage. So if you don't mind, I'll just go about my morning's business so Harry and I can be together this afternoon. Good day, Mr. Jacoby."

The words came fast and at the end she didn't bother to smile, which I appreciated. There was something funny going on below the surface, but it was clear the lady had class, even if she did spill out a lot of her troubles to a total stranger. I wondered about that, but decided she'd gotten to the point where she didn't care who knew. I mumbled an apology and started back in the direction of town.

I never got farther than the next couple of houses, though. Stopping behind a hedge, I waited and watched as Mrs. Ward drove off in a long gray station wagon. Whatever was eating her, you could bet it had something to do with that blonde at the track.

Thinking of blondes reminded me of Ward's son. It was time to get to Cissy's parents already, but as long as I was here, I figured I might as well see if he knew anything. In two minutes I was back up past the flagpole and the pillars, ringing the bell, and in three I was facing Harry Ward over the doorsill.

"I'm sorry to bother you," I lied. "I was wondering if I could use your telephone for a local call. I didn't want to hold your mother up, and I was halfway down the block before I remembered that my sister dropped me off here and I don't have a car."

Luckily for me, he hadn't heard anything of my conversation with his mother. Or maybe these days kids are extra nice to people their parents are sore at. Anyway, he dropped back over the doorsill and motioned me in.

"The phone is in the den," he said, leading me through the living room I had glimpsed last night and on to a long sunny back room with a big picture window. Through it, you could see a lawn that stretched down to the water. He pointed to the phone and went back to a pile of rope he'd been fiddling with on the living room floor. I could see him watching me through the door.

I called my apartment and wasn't too surprised when nobody answered. I let it ring for a while anyway, and looked at the pennants and trophies on the shelves above the white wicker furniture. A small loving cup filled with pencils sat on the telephone table. It was engraved "Third Prize, Class B Regatta, Crab Harbor Yacht Club, 1975."

Six rings seemed enough. I drifted back into the living room.

"Nobody home yet," I said. "Stupid of me to just show up here without an appointment."

Young Ward was polite enough not to agree with me. He shrugged and kept working intently on his nest of ropes.

"I saw the trophies in the den. Are you the sailor of the family?"

"I *try* to be," he answered with unexpected irony. "Father left everything in such a damn mess when he took the boat up for the winter, it was a miracle I got it into the water at all. It's typical," he added, managing to sound both pompous and petulant at the same time. "I'm always the one who has to take care of things."

I must have looked blank, because he put down

the knot he was untying to give me his full attention. His voice deepened into a surprisingly good imitation of his father's pear-shaped tones.

" 'Harry,' " he mimicked, " 'clear this away for me, won't you? I've just had an urgent call from the hospital and I haven't time to do it myself. Patients always come first, you know.' " He turned back to his knot and shoved it onto a growing pile of neat coils. Another talker. It must run in the family.

"And Mother," he sighed after a moment, suggesting untold levels of squalor that were only barely masked by the tailored suit and neatly-tied hair. "But that's different. *Somebody* has to help her out while Dr. Feelgood is out saving the world." He looked up at me almost defensively. "She depends on me a lot."

Both of Harry Ward's parents had struck me as being on the neat side, and I was more than a little amused by his view of his own importance. I was tempted for a minute to ask how mama managed to brush her teeth by herself all those months while sonny was away at prep school, but then it occurred to me that maybe he thought she didn't. No point in picking a fight. Not with those shoulders.

"Well, at least you've got a few days off to work on the boat," I ventured instead. "I guess your folks must like it when you're home on vacation."

It seemed like a neutral thing to say, but he

picked it up with the same nervous irony that seemed to be his way of treating everything.

"Some vacation," he muttered, more to himself than to me. He put the last of the ropes in a blue canvas bag, pulled the string, and turned to me. "Do you know that I've been to a debutante party every night since Saturday?" he demanded. "I've seen more of the waiters at the Plaza lately than I have of my own father. Mother's always in bed by eleven, but now she waits up for me. My welcoming committee." His voice trailed off, and then he changed the subject abruptly.

"What's your niece's name?"

"Lisa Rifkin," I said. It happened to be the truth. "Do you know her?" I doubted it, since the farthest she'd ever been from her home in Phoenix was a riding camp in Colorado last summer, but I was strangely relieved when he shook his head. Harrison Ward struck me as the kind of guy who was much too handsome not to be aware of it. I was frankly surprised there wasn't a sweetie or two hanging around—but maybe they were all still sleeping off their parties.

I flapped my mouth for a while on how worried her mother was, not knowing where Lisa was or who she was with half the time. The kid heard me out, but he didn't look too interested. He looked up when I mentioned Cissy Holder as my niece's pal, but only briefly. "Your niece was running around with her?" he asked. Then he shrugged. "I knew her in the fifth grade. Life was easier then, when your parents could always make everything better. But I guess little Cissy got messed up just like everyone else.''

I thought about defending Cissy's honor, then figured the hell with it. I wasn't going to waste any more time here. I asked the kid if he knew when his father would be back, but he seemed to be no wiser than his mother and even less interested, if that was possible. A clock chiming in the hall gave me an excuse to leave—time to meet my ride at the corner.

Harry walked me to the door and apologized for not having been able to give me a lift himself— something about meeting his mother. He waved as I headed down the walk, and I tipped my hat before I remembered I wasn't wearing one.

Chapter 8

It was about ten blocks from Ward's to the Holder place. As I walked over I considered the possibility of winding things up there and then. After all, there was no reason to suppose the girl hadn't just gone home. Or maybe her parents had kidnapped her and were holding her captive. The house looked like a prison, all right, with all that stone and those little windows, like it was still the dark ages.

There were no distress flags hanging from the tower, anyway. I decided I'd better go inside. I took off my sunglasses and climbed the three short steps to the front door.

The buzzer started Big Ben ringing off in the distance. While I was waiting for someone to answer, I tried to figure out the story in the vertical row of stained glass windows next to the door. Either a guy was knighted, killed a dragon, and rescued a lady from drowning, or else he drowned a lady, killed a dragon, and then was

53

knighted. It depended on which end you started from. No matter what, the dragon got his.

"Yes?"

It was a middle-aged black woman wearing one of those old-fashioned satin maid's uniforms with white trim.

"Hello," I said. "Is Mrs. Holder at home? My name is Quentin Jacoby." I thought I'd try the straightforward approach. Before the maid could answer, an eager voice drifted down from upstairs.

"Who is it, Sylvie? Isabel, is that you?"

The maid stepped back to answer, and I followed her in before she could shut the door. She didn't like it, but she didn't say anything. I looked around.

The front hall was as big as my living room, with dark paneling and a Chinese carpet on the floor. There was a long narrow table on one side, and a statue of what looked like a very old, very fat, bare-bellied Chinaman next to the stairs. Beyond, I could see the real living room, with a huge carved fireplace flanked by a pair of yellow velvet sofas.

"Mr. Jacoby is here to see you, ma'am."

"Ja? Co? By?" the voice repeated, making each syllable a question. "I don't know anyone named Jacoby."

It seemed like a good time to interrupt. I had already decided on my story.

"I'm from the school, Mrs. Holder," I called,

trying not to shout. "I came to talk about your daughter."

"Oh." Wherever the voice was coming from, it had lost its animation. "Well, I'll be down soon."

"Won't you wait in here?" the maid asked, leading me down two steps and into the living room. She watched me settle on one of the yellow sofas, then turned and left.

It was an L-shaped room, and the fireplace took up most of the short leg of the L. There was another big sofa at the other end of the room and a lot of upholstered chairs and low tables grouped together here and there on the thick white carpet. By one wall stood a glass-doored cabinet full of china birds and animals. I saw a blur of pink through the far window and realized that must be the tree the girl had hidden in with her radio. Hecht had said it was about a year ago. I was just getting up for a closer look when I heard someone come in behind me.

I don't know what I was expecting Cissy's mother to be like, but it sure wasn't a doll on the model of the early Lana Turner. She had dark blonde hair and the kind of skin that suddenly makes sense of that old saying about peaches and cream. Her dress was knit like a sweater and was clingy enough to get your imagination going. All of a sudden I decided to sit down again.

She didn't seem to mind my reaction, because she gave me a slow smile and said something about a message for Sylvie.

When she went toward the hall, I could see that the view from the back was just as nice. Then she came back and sat down on the couch about a foot away from me. This was a woman who liked to play with men. I can't say I minded the game.

"You say you're from the school?" Mrs. Holder asked. "I've talked to Dr. Clarke, of course, but I don't believe we've met before." She sent over another of those smiles that hinted she'd been waiting forever to meet me. But at least she'd reminded me of what I was doing there. I straightened up and got to work.

"I'm on the guidance staff," I explained earnestly. "We're starting now to plan for the fall, and I thought I'd discuss with you how Cecilia is doing. Is she here now?"

"Here?" Mrs. Holder gave a little laugh of amazement. "Why, no. It's very sweet of you to come by, but I explained to the headmaster when Cissy withdrew from classes that she was going to need special care. She's sick, you know."

She gave me a look that dared me to contradict her, and then the dreamy smile again. When she smiled, she sort of tilted her head back in a way that was not at all bad. She didn't exactly go with the house, but you couldn't fault Holder's taste. She went on, half closing her eyes as though she were remembering something she had dreamed.

"Cissy is staying at a small clinic in Mount Vernon. She needs private care and she has a wonderful nurse there who's with her all the time.

She ran away, you know, and it was so fortunate that Miss Bronovitch found her. That's the nurse's name—Wanda Bronovitch—but she's very American, you know, really all right, and she handles Cissy so much better than I ever could."

Mrs. Holder gave another little laugh and leaned over confidentially. Her perfume was wonderful. "I'm afraid I'm not really meant to be a parent," she confessed. "Cissy and I have always been more like sisters than mother and daughter, and these last few years—well, I suppose you could almost call it sibling rivalry."

She paused, and there was a shade too much calculation in her fluttering glance. Or maybe I'm just not used to being seduced. Anyway, she changed the subject, but good.

"You know," she said, "I've always liked a cleft chin in a man. I'm surprised we haven't met before. Have you been at Edgewater Day School long?"

"Just a few weeks. I was going over old records and found your daughter's file. I suppose I should have checked with the, er, the headmaster before coming out here. I hope you won't turn me in for bothering you like this." It had occurred to me that it would be a less than great idea for Mrs. Holder to have a chat with the school about its over-eager staff.

I had a good fifteen years on the lady, but she leaned over and patted my hand like I was a little kid. "Don't worry," she cooed. "I won't tell on

you." Then she turned and stared off at the hall.
"I don't know where Sylvie is with the ice," she
said petulantly. "I do like a cocktail before lunch.
And you must join me, Mr. Jacoby. A lady really
can't drink alone."

Sylvie finally showed up with the ice, but three
vodka martinis didn't make Mrs. Holder's smiles
any more instructive. Whatever she knew about
her daughter she wasn't admitting, and it seemed
a good idea to leave before she decided I was
getting too nosey.

It was already way past noon when I left the
house, but Hecht could wait. I looked around the
neighborhood a while, but the only interesting
thing I found was a good deli near the corner of
Palmer Avenue and Weaver Street. Their roast
beef on pumpernickel with Russian dressing kept
the trip from being a total loss. The guy behind
the counter had an aunt who lived in Co-op City
and he told me where I could pick up the express
bus to get me home. The only trouble was, the
bus stop was a mile and a half down scenic Route
One. Public transportation is not so great in the
great American suburbs. Still, I figured I'd better
touch home before seeing Wanda.

Chapter 9

Peter Hecht wasn't parked outside my door the way I'd half expected him to be, so I took that as the first sign to keep moving. The second sign was that I knew where to go. I hadn't really believed Wanda Bronovitch existed, but there she was in the phone book, at an address on 278th Street in Mount Vernon.

The place turned out to be a huge gray frame house with a sign on the lawn that said Cranwood Convalescent Home. With one thing and another, it was almost six o'clock by the time I finally found the place, and if it hadn't been for the light over the sign I'd probably still be looking. There didn't seem to be any separate dormitory, so I just went in the front.

Inside, the building had been partly gutted and redone with lots of turquoise plastic chairs and potted plants. The girl at the desk was poring over a magazine with pictures of brides all over it. Over her shoulder I could see a young guy wearing pajamas and a robe working at a jigsaw puzzle, and an older woman watching television.

"Excuse me," I said, leaning over the desk. "You know where I can find Miss Bronovitch?" I thought about giving a winning smile, like the detectives always do in the movies, but dropped the idea when I saw that the girl wasn't looking up.

"You the relative of a patient?"

"No. Just the friend of a friend."

She flipped to an ad for fancy dishes. "Wanda's on duty now, but she'll be off at eight if you want to wait." She gestured behind her back toward the TV room, but I took a chair by the door.

The place was quiet and the room was hot, and I was beginning to doze when I heard the girl at the desk calling in a low voice, "Wanda, there's a man to see you. He says he's a friend."

I turned around, then jumped up so fast I almost kicked over a cigarette stand. Wanda Bronovitch was the woman from the track, the one who had been arguing with Ward. Only now she was all dressed up in nurse's whites with her hair up under a cap. They were both staring at me. I decided it was time to try out that winning smile.

"Not exactly a friend," I conceded jovially. "At least, not yet. More a friend of a friend." I thought fast, rearranging my ideas to fit in this new connection. "Eli Ward asked me to look you up," I said finally. "About Cissy Holder."

"Cissy Holder? Eli sent you to talk about her?" She seemed astonished, and puzzled too.

"That's right," I answered confidently. "I was hoping I could talk to you for a few minutes. Or better yet, can I take you out to dinner?"

"Dinner?" she said. "I usually eat here . . . in the dining room."

"But a beautiful spring night is not a time for usually," I burbled, drawing her away from the desk and toward the door. Prince Charming in a double-knit sports jacket, that's me.

She wasn't to be drawn quite so easily, though. She stood there for a long minute, obviously sizing me up, before, "All right," she agreed hesitantly. "I guess I've got some messages for Eli myself. There's a Greek restaurant down the block, if that's okay. I have to be back soon."

The girl at the desk had already gone back to organizing her trousseau. All she needed now was a groom.

As we walked over to the restaurant, I trotted out my story about being a guidance counselor at Cissy's school, leaving the details vague enough so that it could seem like I thought the kid was at the convalescent home or like I knew she wasn't.

Wanda went for the second option.

"Sure, I know Cissy," she said. You could see she was still trying to figure me out. "She was at the home for about ten days, early last month. But I don't know where she is now. It was an overdose of sleeping pills, you know." I nodded, and Wanda went on.

"They recuperate fast at that age, but her

parents wanted to keep her in the hospital as long as possible. I don't think she and her mother get along very well. But I guess that's the story with a lot of the kids at these fancy schools, huh?" I just kept on nodding.

We had arrived at Zorba's by this time. I made a fuss about ordering flaming saganaki while I thought out the rest of my story. I started in on a bit about how parents paid a good part of their money to private schools just so they wouldn't have to check up on their kids, but Wanda interrupted me before I got very far.

"You're not really from any school," she announced with finality. "Why did Eli send you to me?"

She eyed me appraisingly. At least I wasn't going to have to sit through any bull about my nice cleft chin. Not with this lady.

"Got me," I said, raising my hands a little off the table. "I'm with the juvenile court. The girl's been skipping parole, and I was hoping you could help me find her. Dr. Ward suggested you might. We try to get the nice ones before they stop being so nice."

I thought about the subway. The purse snatchers and fare jumpers and shake-down artists I used to take to juvenile court had stopped being nice a long way back. Maybe that was why they got so little time. No use even trying to rehabilitate those monkeys.

Wanda sat there shaking her head. She was still

wearing her little nurse's cap, and it bounced more and more on its bobby pins as she got madder and madder.

"I thought you were supposed to be a friend," she said sarcastically. "A friend of a friend, wasn't that what you said? You cops just won't leave me alone, will you? It's two solid days you've been bugging me. All I'm doing is trying to do my job and keep my nose clean, but the whole world is against me. It's not easy being a woman alone, you know. Did you ever think how maybe I'm the one who needs protecting?" She clutched her hands dramatically, then reached over the back of her chair and pulled something from the pocket of her jacket.

"Look at that!" she demanded.

At first I thought it was a telegram. Yellow paper, with a line of words printed on white pasted in the middle of the sheet. Then I saw that the words were cut out of a newspaper. Five of them.

"I—Know—Who—You—Are."

"I don't get it," I said. "Who you are? What's that mean?" But she was obviously regretting the impulse that had made her show me the message in the first place, and she snatched it back.

"Never mind," she snapped. "Forget the whole thing. Go back to your juvenile court. I don't know anything about Cissy Holder. I don't know anything about those other girls on the street. Nothing. So just leave me alone, can't you?"

"So Cissy Holder is one of the girls on the street?"

Wanda looked up, suddenly panicky. "No! No. It's just . . . all these things happening at once." She picked up her fork and started stabbing holes in a piece of feta cheese. "I've got to get back to work," she muttered. "I'm doing double shifts this week."

I could imagine why. As much as Wanda wanted to stay away from Eurydice Avenue, that was as much as I wanted to go there. But I didn't have a warrant. I didn't even have a license. Trying something I saw on TV once, I covered her hand with mine.

"Sure, honey. Let's cut the business short. Mind if next time I call, it's for pleasure?"

She snorted in a way that made me feel pretty foolish. So much for television. It was the second time today a younger woman had treated me like a kid. If this was what they meant by a second childhood, I didn't like it one bit.

After I left Wanda at the nursing home I walked all the way across town, back to where I'd last seen Cissy Holder. There was an extra cop on the beat, but no sign of the girl and no trace of Peter Hecht either. I decided to call it quits. My first day on the job, I had logged thirty miles, met three very interesting ladies, and picked up a lot of confusing information. At this rate, I was going to be no threat to Sam Spade. Or even Nancy Drew.

Chapter 10

It was nine-thirty by the time I got home, showered, and changed into the kind of clothes you can wear around here without being asked whose wedding you're going to.

Nine-thirty. Too late to get out to the track, too early for the late show, and I still hadn't had dinner. No word from Hecht, either. If my phone had been ringing, Mrs. Farbelstein would have made it her business to let me know. So let him find me.

I went down two flights and pushed Sam Fuentes's buzzer to see if he'd be interested in eating. Sam likes to talk a lot about boozing and chasing ass, but daytime TV and a meal that's not too hard on the teeth are more like the real story. We're a real pair, Sam and I.

While he put on his shoes, I studied the painted-on-velvet picture of John and Robert Kennedy that was tacked over the daybed. Sam followed politics the way some people followed ball teams, and he'd been an ardent fan of the Democrats before he'd switched his sympathies to the Puerto Rican Separatists. If anyone ever wants to know the mood of the Spanish community in New York, he should forget his surveys and his educated predictions and just ask Sam. Fifty years on the street peddling those damned sno-cones and Sam was a living repository of every trend that had ever swept the barrio of this northern suburb of San Juan.

Those same fifty years had broadened his taste, though. He made no complain when I steered us over to Goldbaum's Kosher Restaurant. Goldbaum's is the kind of joint that caters mostly to off-duty cabbies, retired fitters and corset makers, and aged Communists who are still looking for the gleam of revolution in the shine on a helping of stuffed cabbage. A nice quiet place.

I had finished my borscht with a roll and was thinking about the chicken-liver special when Sam started waving and shouting across the room in the ridiculous mixture of Spanish and English obscenities he uses for his special friends and favored relatives.

"Hey, Carlos, baby, *marica*, shake your black ass over here. Come here to meet my good amigo"—this was a beam in my direction to show me I was picking up the tab—"my very good amigo, Mr. Quentin Jacoby, who was for many years the man on the subway, but who I am still proud to have meet you because you are such an honest boy with a good steady job that makes your mother so proud."

The object of Sam's attention said something to the three girls he'd come in with and strolled reluctantly over to our table. Sam turned to me, still waving and pointing with his left hand. "This big beautiful *hombre* is Carlos Washington," he announced. "Direct great-great-great-great-grandson of the President Washington, Right, baby?"

I found out soon that Carlos was Sam's nephew, the son of his youngest sister who had become a nurse and married the sergeant of a black platoon during the war. Right then, though, all I could figure was that Sam was somehow claiming not only an acquaintance but even a relationship with what looked to me like an apprentice pimp—a tall, skinny young black man with Valentino sideburns, wearing a sharp pink jumpsuit and a wide-brimmed hat with a snakeskin band. Lord only knows what had brought him into Goldbaum's in the first place, but he sure was regretting it now, because whatever his act was, Sam was for certain ruining it.

"Hey, man, keep it *down,*" Carlos said, pushing his arm palm down and away from his body, as though he could shove away Sam's voice. "Keep it *down.*"

If he had thought coming over would end the noise, he was too late. The three girls had oozed out the door at the first shout. I suggested he join us.

He inspected the chair and apparently decided

it was good enough for his baby-pink gabardines, because he did sit down. There was a twenty-second pause while he ran through some faces that showed his disgust at being with us instead of with the girls; then he turned to me very deliberately and introduced himself.

"Good evening, my man. I am the Sheik."

At this Sam started cackling and telling me about his loco nephew who wanted to act like some kind of film star or numbers runner or who knows what (and here Sam stopped to give us each a mighty poke in the ribs before going on at greater speed), but who was still the wonder of the age because he was so good to his mother and because he had such a wonderful job at Bronx River Hospital in Mount Vernon where he could work inside all the time and not have to be out in the sun. Sam and I used to argue a lot about which was better, working underground or out on the street, and of course we each favored the side we knew nothing about.

There was a lot more about how his nephew was the most important orderly in the whole hospital, just barely below the chief surgeon, but what really came out of Sam's ravings was that the fancy suit and the sharp hat and even the girls had very little to do with the ordinary life of a young man who during the day answered to the name Carlos Leroy Washington. The greatest proof of young Carlos's good nature was the fact that he didn't slit the old man's throat then and there.

Just to shut Sam up, I asked the Sheik the first thing that came into my head, which was if he knew a Dr. Eli Ward who was on the staff at the hospital.

He froze. "Maybe," he answered real slowly. That was when I decided Sam's nephew was perhaps more interesting than he had seemed at first. The good gumshoe never overlooks a possible lead. I learned that from reading "Dick Tracy."

Down at the Police Academy they taught us about something called the open question. That's what you use when you don't want the person you're asking to know you don't know what you're talking about. I tried one out on the Sheik.

"Is Ward the same kind of doctor he is a horse-player?"

The Sheik bit. "Nah, not no more. Abortion, it's legal now. No bread it in anymore, my man. Too bad for Ward. He had a lot of lights-out business one time. All those rich little pieces of pussy coming to him with their *problems*." He said the last word with heavy sarcasm.

That was a surprise. An interesting surprise. I didn't know what to make of this Ward guy, but I noticed that things kept on leading back to him. Was this another piece of humanitarian activism —or a private scam using the counseling as a built-in referral service for an abortion mill? And what was he up to now? Maybe running a little narco clinic? Was that where my friend Cissy was these days?

I'd been letting down my side of the conversation while I puzzled this over, but it didn't matter much because Sam had started in on how we should hit the taverns while the night was young and the juicy *pollos* were still out for the plucking. Fishing out my wallet to pay for dinner, I decided to go back to the other kind of fishing, and turned to Sam's nephew again.

"Tell me," I asked, trying not to sound too interested, "is it true what I hear about there being a lot of new girls down at the Raceway? Seems to me I've been hearing that the best meat running at the races ain't in a sulky these days. A sharp stud like you must have to fight them off."

I had indeed found the right bait. The Sheik gave us twenty minutes of his exploits with the girls while we walked over to the bar Sam had decided had the cheapest Corona beer around. Sometimes I could hardly follow his mix of Spanish and English jive, but I got the drift all right. Black, white, Latino—name it and claim it, the Sheik said. And he'd had them all. The girls, *chiquitas* he called them, would come to the track to pick up a winner looking to celebrate, but if business was slow, a lot of them were out for their own good time, and sweet ladies far and wide knew that the Sheik was their *hombre*. Tonight, he claimed, he was taking it easy—had to rest up from all the demands. As for the new talent, maybe the younger *chiquitas* were a little more businesslike, but he didn't think it would be long before they grew up to appreciate real machismo and started knocking on his door like all the others. I leered appreciatively and held open the door of Tony's Cantina.

Chapter 11

I am not what you could call a heavy drinker, and after three Coronas the Sheik and I were great buddies. By that time we'd finished with the girls at the track and he was telling me all about his stakeout of one Isabella Velasquez, a nurse who worked the night shift at Bronx River Hospital and was worth waiting up for. Sam had long since fallen asleep in the corner of the booth. At one point his nephew turned the old man's head so he wouldn't snore so loud.

The Sheik's stories were making me feel like a case for the nursing home myself, so I countered with a slightly embroidered version of my teenage pickup at the track. It didn't sound right saying I had just dropped the girl off on Eurydice Avenue, so I made like it had been the romance of the century. It sounded so good I got to feeling really sorry for myself and started wailing about how I couldn't find her, how the true love of my life had been swallowed by the naked city. Needless to say, I had completely forgotten about Peter Hecht.

Then I started getting mad. What bum took her away from me? Who had kidnapped her? I would kill him, was what I would do. I took out my wallet to show the Sheik my pistol permit and there was Bea's picture. All of a sudden I started crying.

The Sheik had been quiet ever since I'd mentioned Eurydice Avenue and now he got real solemn.

"Oh, no, my friend," he mourned. "Oh, no. Stay away from that girl. They find you before you find her, and then—big trouble."

He spoke slowly, the way people do when they're more than a little drunk, but still sober enough to care how they sound. But that was okay. I was listening pretty slowly too.

"Whadda ya mean?" I demanded, not really caring. I was getting steamed up again. "I'd like to see anybody keep me from finding that girl if I want to. Listen, buddy," I insisted, "I find little kids their mothers lose on the way home from the beach. I find wallets that get lost off the Times Square shuttle and turn up an hour later on the Flushing line—sometimes I even find the guy who helped the wallet get lost. I find punks who sneak under the turnstile and I spot the hopheads before they get on the train. I can find anything and anybody. Period."

At this point Sam woke up and started singing "Love Is Where You Find It," and we all got up to go. The Sheik walked with us as far as the corner, singing along, but just before we split up, he put his hand on my shoulder.

"You're an all right gringo, my man, and a brave lover. But stay away from Eurydice Avenue. Remember what they did to your friend Dr. Ward when he wanted to stop taking care of the horses." He nodded knowingly and left me to think it over. Which I would have been glad to do, except the pavement had developed a habit of dipping and weaving under my feet. All I could think about was bed. I went off to find it.

Chapter 12

It was Ladies Day at the races, and they were having a special event on the inside track. A footrace. Twice around the oval pushing a silver wheelchair with pink and black silks, and the starting gate was a row of subway turnstiles. As the winner pushed across the finish line, I realized it was Wanda, her hair tucked up under a pink and black nurse's cap. Everyone was cheering and bells were ringing so loud it sounded like New Year's Eve and V-J Day combined. Girls were kissing soldiers everywhere. Then the bells turned into the telephone, and I woke up enough to answer, my head pounding. It was Peter Hecht.

"Sorry to call so early, Mr. Jacoby," he said. "I phoned all day yesterday, but you were never home. It's been two days now since Cissy vanished, and I'm getting jumpy. Did you find her yet, Mr. Jacoby?"

Six-thirty in the morning and already he wanted results. Youth can be so cruel. I considered whether my dream held any new clues, but there didn't seem to be much, except maybe proof that you can take the cop out of the subway, but you can't take the railbird out of the cop.

"Nothing solid," I admitted. "But I'm working on some leads. If you've got nothing better to do today, how about hanging around that hamburger place in Mount Vernon, the one we met at the other night? Maybe your friend will turn up again. But if she doesn't, meet me at the entrance of the Raceway tonight at seven-thirty. And bring money. There should be some fresh horseflesh shipped over from Meadowlands."

I hung up before he could ask for details. I didn't have any to give him. Yesterday I'd been goofing around, playing with the ladies. It was time to start earning my fifty. If only I had a better idea now.

Anyway, I was up now . . . might as well get moving. The morning trio of shower, shave, get dressed. That helped some—at least my head was down to normal size. I walked to Maybelle's and looked over the *Daily News* while I ate my toasted English with cottage cheese. I don't really like the *News* all that much, but at least it doesn't go after that Saratoga thoroughbred crowd. The *News* knows that its readers put Friday's rent money on Thursday night's nag, so they take the whole thing seriously. They know the trotters are life, not art. I used to check out the *Times* for the charts, but reading all those articles about the Wall Street and Fifth Avenue crowd with their midget South American jockeys got to be bad for my blood pressure. Brushing the crumbs from my knee, I circled Fearless Fosdick in the fifth and headed out for my own private think tank, the Coney Island local.

It was a beautiful morning, already warm, and I enjoyed the walk over to the station. The fruit stand under the platform had two big tubs of daffodils, a dollar a bunch, and the damp asphalt by the curb was giving off that special smell of tar and possibility that signals spring. The Korean guy who runs the fruit stand saw me linger and came running over to point out the beautiful asparagus. I nodded appreciatively and climbed the stairs to the station platform.

Waiting for the train, I savored the idea of the twenty-one stops that would take me out of the Bronx and all the way down the length of Manhattan Island. Just before we got to the end of the line I would change to the Myrtle Avenue local to Coney Island, out where Brooklyn meets the sea. Three boroughs for fifty cents isn't a bad deal, though I can remember when the same ride was a nickel. Not that I've got anything to beef about. As a former knight of the underground, I ride free.

On a day like this, even the rooftops of the Bronx looked good. I got to admire them for a good ten minutes before the train pulled in.

As per usual the cars were completely covered

with spray paint graffiti, which the city is paying somebody millions to wash off. It occurred to me as I got on that a city like New York, with all its subway cars, probably keeps the spray paint business in the black single-handedly, and at the same time hires maybe more people than the entire population of Fort Lee, New Jersey, to clean the stuff off. So these punks who hang around the platforms at 3 A.M. to deface the cars because they've got no jobs and nothing to do are probably creating and supporting whole industries. I took out a pencil to see if I could figure it out in numbers, but I still hadn't finished when it was time to change trains.

The Fulton Street station was full of kids: little black kids in YMCA tee-shirts, all with name tags. A couple of hard-boiled-looking counselors were trying to keep them from pushing each other onto the tracks, and I had a nightmare vision of how cozy it would be if we were all traveling to the beach together in the same unventilated car. But then they all trouped upstairs for a tour of the fish market or a walk across the Brooklyn Bridge or whatever it was that had brought them this far downtown.

The Myrtle Avenue train pulled in and I checked it out from force of habit, but there was only an old lady with the regulation shopping bag full of junk, and two kids with bamboo fishing poles. Pretty slim fare for a real nice day. Unemployment must not be as bad as they say.

I settled in for what I hoped would be a nice slow trip, with maybe a good long delay at Prospect Park if I was lucky. Take it from me, there is nothing like a long trip on a hot subway to help you sort out your ideas.

The only trouble was, I didn't have many ideas to sort out. Was Cissy Holder's disappearance tied up with this Ward character? And if so, how? From what I'd seen of her family and heard about her friends, anybody who helped her hole up and pretended like he knew from nothing was doing her a favor.

But then what about Sam's nephew and all his hinting about how maybe the good doctor wasn't so good? Did he know what he was talking about, or was that just something that went with the image, like the phony name and the flashy clothes? And the dark hints about "they"? Every two-bit punk I'd ever known liked to pretend to secret knowledge about big bad guys and heavy deals going down. Ward's wife seemed to think his problem was that he was *too* good, or at least too good to live with. Always running off on some errand of mercy, leaving his own family to sit up nights wondering if he'd ever get home.

And what about those other girls, the ones who'd gotten murdered and dumped nearby? I'd told the kid it was just a coincidence, those bodies turning up on the same street his sweetie had been hanging out on, but how could it be? Was Cissy Holder in a bag somewhere, waiting for the next curbside collection? I'd turned up a lot of dirt in the last forty-eight hours, but none of it stuck together. I spat on my hands and tried to see if I could make mud pies.

I played with ideas about racing syndicates and unlicensed abortion mills and even spent a pleasant five minutes stalled outside the Flatbush Avenue station imagining Mrs. Holder as a high-class hooker who had booted her daughter out of the house to learn her trade from the street floor up. It didn't seem too likely, though. That dame was not the type to know a lot about the work ethic.

I got back to duller, more obvious possibilities. Like maybe Cissy had just taken it into her head to walk out of that convalescent home. It hadn't looked like a maximum security place. And maybe Wanda had taken her in—Peter Hecht had said she'd answered the door at Eurydice Avenue, and the papers had talked about her as the woman who rented the place. And then, when Cissy had vanished from there, Wanda had called Dr. Ward instead of the parents. That would explain what they had been doing together Tuesday night. It was pretty clear Wanda didn't have the highest opinion of Mr. and Mrs. Holder. But how did Wanda know Ward in the first place? And what about that "letter" she'd shown me? "I—Know—Who—You—Are." It was hard to imagine Wanda Bronovitch as an alias, but who knew? What a jerk I was to have come on so strong last night—if I'd been more tactful she might have told me more about it. Any more screw-ups like that and it would be time for me to stop being cute and join forces with the real police.

Some more passengers were getting on at King's Highway. The old lady had gotten off long ago, but the boys with the fishing rods were still there, joined now by a bunch of greasy high school kids loaded down with paper bags of suntan oil and beer. The girls had those teased hairdos that'd gone out of style everywhere else fifteen years ago but were still holding their own in Brooklyn. A raucous crowd, but no trouble-makers. No excuse for not getting back to my own business.

Instead of thinking about Cissy Holder, though, I started daydreaming about the ads printed above the seat. It's another world in those ads, a world where healthy-looking couples improve their sex life by smoking low-tar cigarettes, where potato chips come in tennis ball cans, where everyone buys U.S. Savings Bonds and where gum is chewed by smiling monsters with one slab of solid white stuff where their teeth ought to be. I said hello to the picture of the April Miss Subways, who was a clerk-typist interested in acting and had FOR SALE spray-painted across her face.

Which brought me back to Cissy Holder.

Wasn't it possible she had nothing to do with Ward at all? The most likely thing was that she had just plain taken off. Maybe she had a pimp somewhere. If she hadn't when she'd started, a girl like that wandering around looking for a fix was sure to be found by an operator before long. She'd stepped out of the clean-living billboard world where she belonged, and there was no telling where I'd find her now.

Chapter 13

We pulled into the Stillwell Avenue-Coney Island station. End of the line. I got out with everyone else but didn't bother to get off the platform. Years ago, a day at Coney was a beautiful thing. Five cents took you to some fresh air, the boardwalk, a chance to look out at the immensity of the ocean and then look back and see up the skirts of the girls coming down the parachute jump. The trip took maybe an hour or more, with two changes, but it was great all the way—traveling out with a paper bag full of bologna sandwiches, coming back with sand in your hair, rubbing your new sunburn against the wicker seat. An hour was right for a trip of such magnitude. Nowadays you can go to the moon in an hour, but for my money the trip out to Coney was the better deal.

No more, of course. Now it's a bunch of toughs waiting to mug the old people who are too poor or too stubborn to move away. Steeplechase is closed, Luna Park's long gone. Soon there'll be nothing there but the sand. Fine stuff, sand, but there's nothing like a couple of roller coasters to set it off. I bought a candy apple for old time's sake from the vendor on the platform and waited for the train to take me back to town.

The cabman was taking his break, and it was fifteen minutes before he sauntered to the far end of the train and started making getting-going noises into his squawkbox.

I was the only passenger. I got on the second car, just for variety, and found myself facing the subway map. They've changed it some since I retired, simplified it and jazzed it up with lots of primary colors, but there still wasn't much there to hold my attention. I was staring at the place at Queens Plaza where the IND and the IRT lines come together, but I was thinking about Mount Vernon. And Larchmont.

I considered going back to try and find out if Mrs. Holder was as out of touch as she pretended, but I realized I wasn't up for another bout of her brand of love in the afternoon. I couldn't very well go up to Ward and ask him if he were a butcher and a crook. So that left Wanda. I had just decided to pay another visit to my favorite nurse when I felt something cold and metal jab at the back of my neck.

I didn't move. I didn't open my mouth. I just sat there facing the front of the car, cursing myself for a half-assed fool who handed over his brains when he turned in his badge.

This lasted for maybe five seconds. It felt like half an hour. Then the cold metal was replaced by a hot hand and a big snicker.

"Gotcha that time, ol' buddy."

It was Tony Muldoon. I'd worked with him when he was a kid in training, fresh out of the navy, and we'd gotten to be pretty good friends. I'd never gotten used to his practical jokes, though. Apparently the commissioner hadn't either. Eight years on the force and he still hadn't made it to sergeant. Tony's great ambition in life had been to be a frogman in the navy, but some kind of problem with his ears put him in drydock. I used to think the trouble more likely was water on the brain. What kind of a dumb idea was that to jab me in the neck with his radio and nearly give me heart failure?

We talked for a while about this and that, which turned out to be mostly about how Tony's wife was nagging him to death about how she wanted to get a job. Every stop we'd change cars. There were only three cars on the train and it made me feel a little like the pea in the old shell game, but it was a feeling I was used to. A couple of people stopped to ask directions and one old souse wanted to know why Tony hadn't found his wallet yet, a whole week after he'd been rolled. At Prospect Park, Tony ran to collar a couple of juveniles who were trying to sneak under the turnstile. I called goodbye. Tony's a nice guy, but Serpico he ain't.

Chapter 14

You can ride thirty-five miles on the New York City subway system without changing trains. I don't suppose it's more than twenty from Coney Island to White Plains Road and that includes two changes, but it was far enough for me to plan how I wanted to approach Wanda. Being nice had gotten me nowhere, and being with Tony had reminded me how boring a place nowhere was. Maybe Wanda was the type who liked them tougher. Not exactly my line, but I had seen enough "Kojak" to know how people expected a cop to act. Just to be sure, I spread my shirt collar over my jacket lapels, really sporty-like. I hoped. Too bad I didn't have a pinky ring. I got on a Mount Vernon bus.

The day had started early for me, and it was only a quarter to twelve when I got to the nursing home. My best hope was to catch Wanda while she was coming in to work. I figured she'd be due around noon. She might be staying away from Eurydice Avenue, but I didn't think she'd be living at the nursing home, even if that was where she was listed in the phone book. Somehow Wanda didn't strike me as the dormitory type.

It was a residential neighborhood, and in ten minutes the total of passersby was two women on their way to the laundromat, an old man walking a dog, and three underage maniacs on skateboards.

It had been a long time since that English muffin, and my stomach was making like the Boston Pops tuning up. One of the things I have noticed from my long study of television detectives and my even longer contact with the actual animal while serving as one of New York's Finest, Underground Division, is that television detectives never get to finish a meal while a lot of real detectives will let entire boroughs fall to rubble while they polish off another pepperoni wedge. I had just about decided to be real when Wanda finally came around the corner.

She had taken off her nurse's hat and put on a purple nylon trench coat and patent leather slingback pumps. The coat matched her shoulder bag, which matched the shadows under her eyes. She looked terrible.

I stopped leaning against the lamp post and stepped forward to meet her when she was a few doors away from the nursing home.

"Hello, Wanda," I said. "Since we just barely got acquainted last night I thought I make take up a little more of your time." I grabbed her arm in a way I hoped was both tough and sexy. I never learn. "We've got so much still to talk about."

I expected an argument or at least some surprise, but I wasn't prepared for panic. She nearly jumped out of her shoes when I first grabbed her, and she didn't get much of a hold on herself even after she recognized me.

"Let go of me!" she screeched, pulling away and closing her coat more tightly around herself. Then she turned on me.

"Who are you, anyway?" she demanded shrilly. "And don't tell me you're with the juvenile court, because I called a friend there and they never heard of you."

"I told you, Wanda, I'm a friend of Eli Ward."

"Well, if you've seen him lately, you should know he's no friend of mine," she snarled. "Not any more. Not unless he changes his mind."

I had no idea what she was talking about, but I didn't see why I should let her know that. "That's just what I want to talk to you about," I said smoothly.

For a minute she just stood there, studying my face and tapping her fingers on her coat while she pulled herself together. She plainly was not in a mood to trust me, but something finally decided her.

"Okay," she nodded. "Wait a minute while I go in and get someone to take over my shift."

I walked over to where I could see the door, to

make sure Wanda didn't just vanish out the back, but all she did was talk to the girl at the desk and make a short phone call before coming back outside.

"All right," she said when we were out by the street. "What's on your mind?"

"Just a little chat. But private. And honest. Know a place where we can have that kind of talk?"

Wanda paused a minute, then shrugged. "Yeah, I know a place. My car's around the corner."

I nodded and followed her to the car, a yellow VW convertible with terry cloth covers on the front seats and the usual litter in the back. I got in reluctantly. Since the war, I don't patronize products made in Germany, and at no time have I liked cars, but I figured this time I was on a humanitarian mission.

I didn't say anything while we were driving and neither did Wanda, but I wasn't too surprised when we pulled into the driveway of the house on Eurydice Avenue. I just hoped Peter Hecht wouldn't see me and come running out of the restaurant. If he was still there.

Either he wasn't or he didn't. Wanda dug out her keys and let us both into the house, switching on the hall light as she closed the door behind her.

"I'm having a drink," she announced. "Do you want one?"

I gauged the vacuum where the English muffin

had been and thought how this really wasn't a good idea, but then I remembered my new image.

"Sure, honey. Whatever you're having."

She vanished into the kitchen, and I had a chance to look around. If I was hoping for signs of Cissy Holder, there weren't any. For that matter, there weren't many signs of Wanda, either. At some point the place had been remodeled with lots of cheap wallboard and a built-in fish tank where the gas logs in the fireplace used to be. The effect was dreary and anonymous. I couldn't tell what the upstairs was like, but the building was flimsy enough to convince me that if there had been anyone up there, I would have heard him breathing. The first floor was fitted out like a separate apartment, with a daybed in what once had been the dining room. The place was real dark. The sun had no chance to get in.

The furnishings were standard cheapo. A balding shag rug, an Indian cotton bedspread, a couple of plastic cube tables in each room. The walls were bare except for a faded psychedelic poster taped up over the bed. It was a picture of a distraught-looking young woman, naked from the navel up. She had masses of curly fluorescent green hair and her breasts were day-glo orange. The tape had come loose in one corner, and the top of the poster curled down over her left eye. It made it look like she was winking.

The front room was dominated by a giant color

TV in its own cabinet, and across from it was a formica dinette set, the kind where the plastic table is supposed to look like wood and the plastic chairs like wicker. The fish tank in the fireplace had a lot of orange pebbles on the bottom and three goldfish swimming around inside. There was a half-eaten carcass of another fish floating on the top. I was just deciding not to look at it when Wanda came in with the drinks.

The decor was strictly teen-age newlywed, but the two martini glasses were more in keeping with her age. I pulled up a dinette chair from the front room and Wanda sat down on the daybed.

"Here's looking at you," she said.

"Here's looking for other people."

Wanda put her glass down on one of the plastic cubes and reached for her purse. She took out a pack of cigarettes, lit one, and turned to me.

"What's that supposed to mean?"

Wanda's small talk was about as original as mine, so I just got to the point.

"What that means is I want to find Cissy Holder, and I think you know where she is." Wanda's eyes narrowed as she took a drag. "Two days ago, I saw her come into this house. She let herself in with her own key. That night somebody left a dead body outside your door, and the next morning you told a friend of mine you'd never heard of Cissy Holder. Yesterday you gave me some cock-and-bull story about how fast Cissy got better and checked out of your nursing home.

Now I know that's not true and you know I know,
so how about telling me where she really is. Or do
I have to get mean?'' I patted my jacket as
though there was something dangerous inside. I
also sucked my gut, just to improve the image.

She decided to play it classy. ''I haven't the
slightest idea what you're talking about, Mr.
Jacoby. That woman they found—it was terrible,
but it can't have anything to do with me. And I
told you, I haven't seen Cissy Holder for over two
weeks.''

She reached for another cigarette, and I
realized what it was about her outfit that had
been bothering me.

''If you haven't seen Cissy for two weeks, why
are you carrying her purse?'' I demanded. ''Sorry
to keep you from your smokes, but I think I'll
just take a look inside there.''

Wanda sat back heavily on the daybed.

''Okay, slugger. Have it your way.''

In half a minute the lady had turned into a moll.
Without taking her eyes from my face, Wanda
handed over the big purple suede pouch with the
beaded fringe. Like the rest of her clothes, like the
furniture in the apartment, it was designed for a
considerably younger woman. And a more
innocent one.

I turned the bag upside down, letting the
contents fall all over the shag rug. Some makeup
rolled under the bed. A wallet fell out, and some
keys on a chain with a yellowed rabbit's foot. A

bottle bounced once and broke when it hit the built-in breakfront. The room began to stink of Tabu.

There was no gun, and I didn't know if that made me feel better or worse. The wallet had thirty dollars, a Blue Cross card, and a Social Security card made out to Wanda D. Bronovitch. The change-purse section had a quarter, three pennies, a beat-up St. Christopher's medal, and a dog-eared betting stub. In other words, nothing. I felt kinda foolish and I must have looked it, too, because Wanda started making fun of me.

"Gee, and she was in there just last night," she sneered. "Or maybe you were looking for a map— X marks the spot. Sorry I can't help the big tough probation officer find his little chickie bird. Except maybe you're not a probation officer, just like you're not a guidance counselor. Maybe you're just a dirty old man who likes to push women around. I don't know why I'm even talking to you, Mr. Whoever-you-are. I have enough people in my life without taking in strays off the street."

She had a point, but this wasn't the time to admire her logic. I countered with my last piece.

"Maybe you're talking to me so I won't start telling other people what I know," I suggested. "Like how you're using this place as a boarding house for your call girls. Are they all at work right now, Wanda?" I needled. She just sat there, tapping her foot nervously on the linoleum. I played my trump. "I could also tell them how chummy you are with Eli Ward. I know a lot of folks who'd be interested in the details of that little fight the two of you had the other night over at the Raceway. And the police are only some of them."

It was pure bluff, but it got to her all right. Only not the way I'd expected. Her eyes glazed over and she started screaming.

Then all hell came through the kitchen door.

Chapter 15

There were three of them, each one bigger than the last. They were probably expecting a shamus out of Hollywood, stripped to the waist with a holster against his hairy chest, leering at the girl whose dress he had just torn from her luscious body. Instead they found old Jacoby, fifty-five and graying, and if I had taken off my shirt there'd be an undershirt with the big armholes that went out of style twenty years ago. It must have let some of the fun out of Osterizing my face, but they tried anyway.

Three interchangeable punks, the kind that breed around the edges of organized crime and grow up on promises of how they'll get to rub out a victim of their very own when they're older. The last thing I saw while my eyes were still working was Wanda grabbing her bag and scramming out the front door.

That was also the last I saw of Wanda's apartment. The next thing I remembered was waking up on the sand. When I tried to move it became clear that my friends hadn't minded hitting a guy while he was down.

I had no idea where I was. But wherever I was, I was alone. In a couple of months every one of the beaches around New York would be crowded until after midnight. For now, though, it was just me and the gulls and the sunset. At least I thought it was the sunset. Maybe it was just the technicolor explosions in the back of my brain. I lay there for another ten minutes trying to decide. At the end I still hadn't made up my mind, but I thought I could lift my head enough to look around me.

The happy trio that had brought me here couldn't have had their hearts in the production, because they did a lousy job. No style, dumping me just over the edge of a parking lot. Any hit man with class would have rolled me up like a hedgehog and left me under the beach grass. It must be hard to find good help nowadays.

After another five minutes I tried looking the other way. That was harder, since it meant turning my head ninety degrees and rubbing sand in a place that didn't want to get rubbed, but I managed. The water looked about a hundred and fifty miles away. I started edging toward it. At least it was downhill.

Several decades later, I arrived. For a while I just lay there and let the little waves wash over the back of my head. Then I edged in further, trying to soak my whole head without drowning. The tide was coming in and each wave got a little more of me. The water must have been about thirty-four degrees. By the time it was turning my ears to ice cubes, I began to feel human. I lay there a while longer just to make sure it wasn't a passing fancy, and then I actually managed to sit up.

It was getting dark for real now, but that was all for the good. I didn't want to see what my face looked like while I washed it off. The salt water stung like hell, and I couldn't stop my teeth from chattering. At least it wasn't a death rattle. I buttoned my jacket all the way to hide the mess that was my shirt and started the long trek back to the parking lot. Except for the time my body decided to sit down, it went pretty well. As far as I could tell, nothing was broken. My dentist might have something to say about my teeth, but he's my cousin and a born complainer since he was a kid.

When I got to the end of the parking lot, a sign told me where I was.

WELCOME TO ORCHARD BEACH
NO DOGS OR ALCOHOLIC BEVERAGES ALLOWED
PLEASE DON'T LITTER

Orchard Beach. That's in Pelham Bay Park. It meant two buses to get home, but it could have been a lot worse. I fished in my pocket and was surprised to find I still had everything I'd started out with that morning. Give or take a few brains. I starting limping to the bus stop.

Chapter 16

It was seven o'clock, the tail end of the rush hour, by the time the No. 12 bus pulled up, but I just settled myself in an end seat and didn't look up till we hit my stop. Hicks from out of town like to talk about how New Yorkers are rude, but in my experience it's a city with real tact. Witness the fact that you can ride a fairly crowded public vehicle at rush hour looking like death on the half shell, and nobody would dream of saying a word.

I got off the bus and mounted the overpass that would take me across the road and around my building. Touching down on the other side, I bought a lemon sno-cone from a younger version of Sam Fuentes. What you're supposed to do when somebody's been goose-stepping on your rib cage is grab a slug of rye whiskey, but what I really wanted just then was an ice pack. A sno-cone was the closest I could come. I slurped down some of the cold mush, trying to ignore the way it felt when it hit my gums. Then I folded over the top and rubbed the paper cone slowly over my face.

That felt good, and a cold shower when I got home felt even better. In a funny way, I liked knowing I could take a beating and still stand up afterward. That's something you wonder about a lot when you're on the force. That and whether you'll have the nerve to shoot to kill. I'd been lucky—I'd never gotten past wondering. Now at least I knew about the first part.

My whole body ached, but I didn't look too bad. There would be lots of bruises across my ribs and thighs in the morning, but nothing I couldn't live with as long as I stayed out of a bathing suit. I also had a black eye and a nasty-looking welt on the side of my chin. For some reason the lump in the back, which felt as big as a cantaloupe, didn't show. After my dumbness in following Wanda to her apartment, my head could use some enlargement.

There was still time to catch the last bus to the Raceway. I figured I might as well keep on being nosey—I must be on to something to get this kind of service. I just had to be more careful. Maybe Wanda would be there, or maybe even Cissy Holder. If she wasn't at home and she wasn't at Wanda's, she had to be somewhere. Or maybe I could follow up the Sheik's hints about Ward and the horses. At the very least, Peter Hecht would be waiting for me. This was one day I felt I had earned my retainer.

I got dressed pretty quickly, considering what agony it was to bend down and put on my socks. At least I didn't have to look like anybody's Park Avenue Uncle Quentin anymore. The boys I'd spent the afternoon with weren't what you could call fashionable. I zipped up my windbreaker, double-locked the door, and headed out.

A detour to the Co-op Superette got me an evening paper and a cup of Mr. Java's special decaffeinated sludge. My mouth was still vetoing the idea of solid food, and my ribs hurt too much to let me notice my stomach.

I trotted the last few feet to the bus stop and staggered on just as they were pulling out. The late bus that connects with the direct run to the Raceway is always full of family men, quiet guys who are staking their bets to pay for the kid's communion suit. I edged the plastic top off my coffee and settled down to read the paper in peace.

Chapter 17

The peace lasted as far as the front page. While I was dragging my ass around Mount Vernon and Orchard Beach, police had identified a body that had washed ashore yesterday at Great Neck, six miles away across the Long Island Sound. A naked woman, strangled, with knife wounds all over her backside and her legs. The only clue to her identity was the track marks on her arms. That and the fact that they had found her inside a green plastic garbage bag. The bag had torn, and one leg was sticking out. I felt sick, but I forced myself to keep reading.

Even dead, Cissy must have had something of that finishing school look, because the homicide people had started with the files on minors, first drug arrest. The story went on for a while, but I was stopped by the photo. It was a three-column picture of Cissy's stepfather and her mother coming out of the morgue. They were wearing tennis clothes, and Mrs. Holder looked bewildered, like she'd just been insulted for no reason at all.

Anyway, the search was over. Special Agent Oy Oy Seven had screwed up and was about to be retired without pension. The NYPD could take it from here, and the kid could get to the funeral on his own. My first and last case as a locator of missing persons had been solved for me by the *New York Post*, and they were welcome to it. I decided to blow a wad on the Perfecta and get drunk in the clubhouse.

Only it didn't work out that way. When I got to the gate, I had no stomach for watching horses run around in circles pulling grown men in little go-carts. I kept on thinking of Peter Hecht staking out the hamburger joint while the girl he was waiting for was getting wrapped around by eels and stabbed at by horseshoe crabs. I remember when I was just starting to work on the trains, before the war, they were doing some repairs where the tracks go under the Harlem River. I was there when they found a body somebody had stuck under water for safekeeping, and I'll never forget the way the thing looked. You couldn't tell if it had been a man or a woman, it was so bloated and chewed up. Not the kind of thing you like to imagine for someone you had had your arm around three days before.

So what could I have done?

I could have saved her, that's all. I could have

gone right up to that house on Eurydice Avenue
and not taken no for an answer, instead of pussy-
footing around Larchmont wasting time and
getting nowhere. I could have gotten some help,
instead of making like the Lone Ranger. That's
what a real detective would have done. I'd spent
too many years weaving through the cars of the
local, keeping my eyes down to look for pickpockets. I'd forgotten how to do things out in the
open. For a minute I was even glad Bea was gone,
so I wouldn't have to tell her about how I'd let a
nice kid down and maybe helped his girl get
killed.

Had I actually done that, butting in and asking
questions and making people nervous? It seemed
like a coincidence, some psycho out for young
girls on the street, but maybe that was just the
way Cissy's friends operated. If they could have
three guys waiting in the kitchen for me, how
many more would they need somewhere else,
doing their number on Cissy Holder?

Then I remembered that the body had been
found before I'd ever gotten to Wanda. So maybe
that explained why those toughs were out for me.
It's one thing to be looking for a schoolgirl and
another to be looking for a stiff.

I hung around the gate for another forty-five
minutes, watching the late stragglers come in and
the early losers slink out. I think I was half
waiting for the kid to show up, wanting him to
tell me that the newspaper was wrong and we

could keep on playing our game of hide-and-seek. But the only people who came up to me were a couple of wash-outs mooching their bus fare home. My kind of guys. Wash-outs.

Then I started thinking about Bea again. We'd had our troubles just like everybody else, especially when I got out of the army and couldn't get my job back for over a year. But Bea was always a fighter. "You gonna let them get away with this?" I could hear her asking in that feisty voice she got when she was trying to pull me out of the dumps. "You gonna let them get away with stomping all over Quentin Jacoby?"

The words seemed to echo in my ears, until I realized that I was saying them out loud. I looked quick around me, but there was nobody listening to the loony talking to himself.

I folded the newspaper, stuffed it in my pocket, and walked back to the entrance gate. The logical thing to do was forget about Cissy Holder. The boys at Wanda's had just wanted to scare me off, not kill me, so if I got lost they'd probably let me stay that way. It would be simple and so safe . . . just call it quits, tell Peter goodbye, go back to my old routine . . . and sit on my butt in my empty apartment waiting for the arrival of the bedpan brigade. Well, sorry fellas, but I wasn't ready for that yet. Cissy hadn't been the first and she wouldn't be the last, unless I did something about it. I reached the gate. I still didn't know what was going on, but it had all started at the

Raceway and it probably came back there, too. If I wanted an inside track on the truth, I'd have to look on the other side of the fence.

Chapter 18

The truth. The truth was that someone had killed Cissy Holder and dumped her body in the drink, wrapped up like yesterday's garbage. The question was who and why? But to find out who had dead-ended Cissy's life I had to know where she had thought she was going.

The route went in stages. There were some connections between Cissy and Wanda, and Wanda and Ward, and, if the Sheik could be trusted, between Ward and some tough guys. If I could figure out what those connections were, I still wouldn't stop the big boys, but at least I might take the thrill out of killing young girls who were maybe getting too well-known.

I had already looked over the racing card that morning, but I checked it again for late changes. I was in luck. The big race was the eighth, a ten thousand dollar purse for pacers. Spots of Time was the favorite, which was no surprise with Art McGill driving, but there had been a last-minute entry. It was Ward's horse, Doctor's Dilemma, with Vince Barsini in the sulky. The odds were sixty to one, but I figured if Ward thought enough of the horse to enter her at all, he would likely be at the Raceway to cheer her on. I'd start looking for him soon, but first there were some other things I wanted to check on.

There are two places to sit down and drink in the clubhouse. I peered into the restaurant first, but there were no familiar faces, so I made for the bar. I wasn't dressed for a party, but that was okay. All I wanted to do tonight was size up the talent. The hostess put me at a small table by the door, and I ordered a Jack Daniels, straight up.

My visit to Wanda had given me some ideas to go with my mangled ribs. If my suspicions were right, Dr. Eli Ward was picking up some loose change as a high-class pimp, finding messed-up girls in the suburbs and bringing them in to work the track. Wanda ran the place on Eurydice Avenue as their crib, using the upstairs bedrooms for the girls. If they worked out okay in Mount Vernon, they were probably taken into Manhattan for some of the classier call girl operations, or maybe even shipped around the country to other cities. No telling how big the market is for guys who basically want to make it with their daughters.

It was a cozy little operation if it worked the way I thought it did. A highly respected doctor, with a wife who looked like the president of the garden club and a son who must be the debutante catch of the season. A member of the yacht club, a lecturer on drug abuse—wouldn't you trust him with your daughter? So you send her for a cure to the nursing home he recommends, and you meet the fine nurse there with the funny name. And you'd never expect you were paying to turn your daughter into a hooker.

If the girl wasn't on the hard stuff when she arrived, it probably didn't take Wanda long to fix that. And then after a little while, the girl could become a special kind of outpatient—watching TV and knitting doilies during the day, hustling the track at night.

For whoever was running the final show, it was a small but steady supply of fresh faces, guaranteed clean and under medical supervision. For the doctor, it was a healthy cut of the take, plus maybe a commission and a promise that the girls would vanish without his having to do anything about them. For the girls, it was a one-way ticket to nowhere, but who cared about them?

And as long as they kept the numbers down, there really wouldn't be much danger. The parents Ward was dealing with had lost touch with their kids long ago. As long as Ward kept telling them that little Debbie or Sharon was doing fine, but would be better off without visitors, the folks would keep on sending money. If they came to visit, there was probably enough hostility from the girls to convince the parents not to come back. And if Debbie or Sharon decided to start a new life in Los Angeles, or Cleveland, or Toronto, and then vanished after a postcard or two—well, that was hardly the doctor's fault, and not the kind of thing a parent likes to talk about anyway. By the time they got around to thinking about checking with the police or a private investigator, it wouldn't be too much of a shock if the girl turned up as a dancer in a topless-bottomless bar on sailor's row. By then she'd be too old for Ward, anyway.

It was all a guess, but it made some sense. All except the killing part. That didn't fit the picture. That was what I had to figure out. I looked around the room. It didn't take long to weed out the trainers' wives, the barflies, the bored mamas downing the daiquiris while their sugardaddies lined up at the fifty-dollar window. I eliminated the middle-aged woman who sat carefully burning her betting stubs in the ashtray. That left a blonde who must have been sewn into her clothes and a Latin type who sure knew how to jiggle to the Muzak. They weren't what I was looking for.

Then there was the girl sitting alone at one of the little tables, drinking something tall and playing with the chain of a necklace that vanished into her low-cut tee-shirt. Brunette, somewhere between baby fat and voluptuous, with the air of someone who was just passing through . . . either she had been left there by her date, or she was the proof of my theory. I picked up my bourbon and walked over.

"Can I buy you a drink?"

She looked up, and I realized why I knew she wasn't a regular at the track. In the few minutes I'd been there, she was the only person in the room who hadn't looked up once to check the races on the closed-circuit screens that ringed the room.

"I'd like a vodka and tonic, thank you."

Her voice was clear and precise, with just a hint of lisp. It was also absolutely dead. Talking to her was like talking to one of those telephone answering machines—they wait for you to finish, but they've already got their next line recorded in advance. After her drink came, I asked her how she liked the races, and she answered she liked a good time on any turf. Was I looking for a good time? she asked. I said sure, and her eyes opened enough to give me that appraising look they learn real fast, deciding whether or not I was a cop. I must have passed, because her next sentence shot right through my guts.

"The Raceway Motel is just across the highway. Fifty dollars regular, one-twenty for anything fancy. In advance. Anything."

She said it like she said everything else, as though it were a memorized speech. It was exactly the same one Cissy Holder had used. I only hoped this kid had more luck holding onto the role.

I mumbled something encouraging and leered toward the men's room, saying I'd be right back. Before I got up, I gave her a long slow feel high up on the thigh, so she'd know I was coming back. That woke her up some, which was too bad. I wasn't coming back at all.

I left a five on the bar to pay for the drinks, and faded toward the partition that hid the men's room. It also hid the service entrance, and that's how I went out.

Chapter 19

I walked past an open closet crammed with dirty linens and another room that looked like where the waitresses changed into their uniforms. The hall stopped at a peeling green fire door that opened onto a dimly-lit metal staircase. I had no idea where I was, but I figured I'd get out eventually. I headed downstairs, thinking about the girl I'd just left.

It wasn't the kind of proof that would mean anything in court, but there was no doubt in my mind that Cissy had been hooked into an operation that specialized in high-class teenage talent. Was Ward running it? The easy way to find out would be to spend some time tailing the people who showed up at the doctor's rap sessions. If I was right, it was easy money I'd spot one or two of the girls at the Raceway within a month or two. But I didn't have a month or two.

I wondered if he had another operation going for boys. That kind of stuff goes over big these days, and some of those high school boys are

mighty good-looking. Look at his own son. Or
Peter Hecht—there was somebody's idea of a
pretty boy.

Thinking of Hecht brought me back to the main
fact—the body they'd fished out of the Sound. At
least no young guys were being carved up and
dumped around town.

I walked faster, the metal stairs clanking and
echoing around me. I realized I'd already passed
a couple of landings. Must be ground level by
now. Time to get out of this erector-set cage and
rejoin the crowds.

Except it wasn't that easy. The first door I
tried was locked, and so was the next. I went back
up three flights to the door I'd come in from, but
that was locked, too. The staircase was one of
those jobs I call a double safety—open from the
inside for an emergency exit, but locked from the
outside to keep just anyone from wandering in.
The last time I'd gotten stuck in one of those was
in a forty-two story office building in Manhattan,
when I'd had the bright idea of trying to beat the
elevator down two floors. Instead I found myself
marching down thirty-nine flights to the second
level of the underground garage—the first door I
could find that would open. It beat me what they
had here to be so protective about, but mine was
not to reason why, as they say in that poem Miss
Blake made us memorize in high school. I turned
around and started clanking my way down to
what I hoped would be eventual liberation.

Five flights later, I did reach a door that opened, but it just led into a tunnel that was as light and airy as the staircase I'd left. It was more a corridor than a tunnel, but somehow it felt underground. I don't know why, exactly—it was just a place with green linoleum floors and yellow cinderblock walls, with perfectly ordinary fluorescent lights in the ceiling. There was something dank about it, though.

The corridor went about thirty feet, and then it dead-ended into a row of dusty metal lockers, their doors hanging open to save me the trouble of even thinking they had anything inside. I had gotten myself into some kind of storage room, but the place looked as though it had been abandoned for years. There were a couple of gap-toothed brooms leaning against the wall, and a pile of filthy paper cylinders in front of one of the lockers.

I unrolled one of the cylinders. It was a poster announcing the track's Diamond Jubilee, July 14, 1973. I threw it back on the pile and dusted off my hands. Nothing of interest here.

I was about to go back up the stairs and try pounding on some of those locked doors when I noticed the ancient set of wooden rungs attached to the wall. I had missed it at first in the shadow of the lockers.

A ladder meant something to climb to. Looking up, I saw that the last four feet of the ceiling, over the lockers, had never been modernized, and that it wasn't a ceiling at all, but one of those old-fashioned cellar doors that lie flat against the ground outside. Parts of the Raceway building go back to the turn of the century, and this must have been one of them. A storage cellar nobody knew what to do with anymore.

I wedged myself in next to the lockers and started climbing. After three rungs I was able to reach the wooden bolt that held together the two sides of the door. I pulled it out, laid it on top of the lockers, and climbed another rung. On the second try, I got one side of the door to flop open.

The ladder wasn't attached to the wall any too firmly, but I risked standing on the top rung. From there I could stick my head out the open side of the door and see where I was. Or I would've been able to, if it hadn't been so dark. I could hear them announcing the fourth race, but it all seemed very far away, like the lights that were glowing somewhere to the left. I reached my hand up and felt around the opening. It was packed dirt. Gingerly, I pulled myself forward until my upper body was on the ground, then stepped off the ladder and into space. I hung there for a moment counting the different ways my ribs were killing me, then lunged forward and got my legs out.

But out where? It took a minute for my eyes to adjust from the fluorescent brightness of the cellar to the night shadows outside. Then I realized where I was. Sam Fuentes's cousin Jorge once hit it big in the numbers and used his jackpot to buy into a standardbred with three other guys. One thing they'd forgotten to figure in was the feed bill, but before they'd lost the nag in a claiming race, Jorge had given me and Sam a tour of the paddocks and the barns, including a glimpse of a little cul-de-sac between the grandstand and the paddocks where some of the out-of-work drivers gathered to smoke and curse their luck. It was just a little empty space, under the end of the grandstand and facing the entrance to the paddock, but the arrangement of pillars and fences and the back wall of the parking lot formed a private little hollow cut off from the bustle of the rest of the Raceway.

But not all that private. I was just reclosing the storm cellar contraption I had crawled through, when I heard voices coming toward me. So I wasn't the last man on earth. I wasn't sure if that was a comfort or a threat. I sat down on the shadow of a pillar to decide.

The voices got louder. One of them was nasal and self-righteous.

"So I should've let him go right from the start, huh?" its owner demanded. "Well, you know what happens with that horse when you let him go? He starts sashaying all over the track and turning over his sulky, that's what happens. Remember Manny Aquilla last year? Broke both his arms and half his ribs, and wouldn't have gotten out of there with his head in one piece if some guy hadn't jumped the rail and pulled him off the course. Yeah, that's what happens when you give him his head. 'Course that wouldn't be no hair outta your ass.''

Through this, the other voice had been mumbling something I couldn't make out. When the driver stopped his whine, I realized it was a single phrase, repeated over and over without any stops between words, the way you talk to quiet a nervous horse. "Awrightpeteawrightpeteawright," his friend said in a monotone. I sneaked a peek: fat and forty, with blubber set off by an orlon knit shirt. As he talked he started pacing, ducking his head to avoid the hardware of the stands above us. He turned back to the driver, tossing away a crushed paper cup that had once held beer. "Awrightpeteawrightpete," he said again, soothingly.

Pete wasn't soothed. Whatever was eating him, he was going to make sure it took a bite out of the other guy, too. His manager, probably. These standardbred drivers are much bigger than jockeys, and stronger, but they don't have the same kind of self-control. Or maybe it's just that they're less obsessed with their bodies. Not having to be on a diet all the time may make you less nervous, but it can give you more of a temper. Lots of energy and very little self-control.

"Awright! Awright!" the driver repeated bitterly. "That's all you know how to say! Well, it's not all right. I ain't got a single race tonight, and if you think that's all right you're fired right now!" He pounded his fist into one of the metal girders on the underside of the stands, then spun around to face his manager.

"That's right," he snarled. "Fired. And I'm through with this hole of a track, too. Freezing my ass here when by rights I should be in Florida." He tore something from his coat and threw it at the manager. "You can just take this and tell those track officials where to shove it for me!"

I didn't feel like getting in the way of that temper, but I needn't have worried. The driver went stomping off toward the parking lot, then veered left in the direction of the clubhouse exit. Blubber boy stooped for a second and shoved something in his pocket, then called after his protégé.

"Hey, Pete," he pleaded. "Come on. Wait up." He rubbed his belly nervously, then trotted off in pursuit. As he left, whatever he had picked up dropped out of his pocket again. It caught the light and glittered briefly as it fell. The fat slob. I felt like making a citizen's arrest for littering, but there was too much else going on.

The fourth race was over, and people were moving down the rail by the end of the grandstand to peer in the entrance to the paddock area. Peering in the door was as close as they could get. The State Racing Commission sees to that, with an armed guard at the door to make sure nobody but drivers, trainers, owners, and other authorized personnel gets in.

Which was too bad for me, because inside was where I wanted to be. There had been no sign of Ward in the bar or restaurant, so my last hope was that he was at the paddock with his horse. I listened to the feet running up and down the stands over my head, then watched my own foot kick at a dandelion clump that had somehow gotten the notion it could grow under there. I pushed around some trash with my toe, and turned over the piece of plastic the fat manager had dropped.

I had struck gold. Rubies. The keys to the city. The glitter was a pin, and the plastic was a card that said AUTHORIZED in red letters. My friend the driver had thrown away his badge.

Blessing his losing streak, I grabbed the magic talisman that would get me into the paddocks.

Chapter 20

Getting in was a cinch. I stuck the badge on my jacket and marched up to the gate. The police guards on duty eyed me quizzically, but I started talking before they could ask me who I was.

"Don't let me bother you, boys," I chortled amiably. "Just have to get at this stuff in here." I waved vaguely at the breathalyzer and some other medical-looking equipment just inside the door. My hope was that they'd take me for some kind of minor track official. Assistant collector of urine specimens was what I probably looked like, but when he saw the badge, the officer just shrugged and went back to his little guard house. Before he could change his mind, I hotfooted through the gate and into the building, past where they were washing down the horses from the last race.

The place was jumping with grooms and drivers and trainers and vets, with a scattering of lab people running back and forth with clipboards

121

and bottle trays. I stopped at a row of empty stalls to catch my breath.

Now that I was in, it was time to start looking around. The girl at the bar was only part of the story. I remembered what the Sheik had been telling me last night, about the way the big "they" didn't like it when Dr. Ward wanted to stop "taking care" of their horses. It was hard to tell how much Sam's nephew really knew, but it was a sure thing that if Ward were working over the horses it wasn't as an osteopath. With all the new drugs coming on the market and all the advance samples a guy like him would be getting, Ward could probably dope up every horse in the park with something different and never have the track vet catch him. Of course, there was nothing to say he was doing his number here, but it made sense that he would be, having a horse here himself and all. I'd put a lot of sawbucks through the window at that track, and the idea that some silver-haired creep with a razor crease in his pants was maybe taking my money without even giving me a chance burned me up. I zipped up my windbreaker and hurried through the paddock, past the place where they keep the sulkies and out into the dark. Somewhere out there, I felt sure, was something that would tie it all together.

They rebuilt the stables at Mount Vernon about fifteen years ago, tearing down the old firetrap barns and putting up a bunch of modern concrete numbers, two stories high with a ramp to lead the horses to the second floor. The whole thing looks like a bunch of little garages, which is maybe what they are, but the management is mighty proud of them.

I started with the first one on the right. The only thing moving was a watchman, and the only thing moving on him was his pulse. He was a grizzled old guy wearing a green cardigan that looked like he'd been born in it. His chair was tilted back against the wall, his feet were up on a gallon can of liniment, and some of his drool had dried where it had dropped on his collar. There were a couple of empty pint bottles next to the liniment can. It didn't look like anybody cared much whether this barn was watched or not.

Just to be thorough, I headed up the ramp to the second story. Sure enough, it was empty. This early in the season a lot of horses are still in Florida or on the farm. Coming out, however, I saw an interesting scene. The barn diagonally across from me was all lit up, and standing at the gate at the top story, silhouetted against the light, was Dr. Eli Ward. He was just there for a second and then he vanished.

Nothing unusual about that. It just meant Ward was more serious about his horse than some owners who like to watch the races from the clubhouse. Once the races begin you can't enter or leave the paddock area, so a lot of people just never come in.

Another five minutes passed. They were announcing the seventh race. There was a clatter of horses in the yard, but nothing more from the other barn. If Ward was going to get his entry into the eighth race, he'd be coming out soon. I waited, staring at the lighted door the way you stare at a TV test pattern when you don't want to believe a station has gone off the air.

Finally they decided to resume the program, but with a change of act. I'd been waiting for a trainer and a racehorse, followed by Ward wearing that special nervous smile you always see on an owner who's been telling himself that this time the nag really will win. I got the first two all right, but the heavy-set guy bringing up the rear wasn't Ward.

It was Val DeLillo, one of harness racing's heavy spenders and a familiar figure to anyone who's ever put in time at the track. A buddy of mine in the Racket Squad had been trying to get his mitts on DeLillo for years, but the only mug shot they'd gotten so far was the news photo from the winner's circle.

No nervous smile for DeLillo. The guy was dressed up like one of the flamingos at Hialeah, which was probably where he'd been last week. Pink shirt, orange and pink plaid sports jacket, white pants, and the regulation white alligator loafers shining in the floodlights as he marched stiffly down into the yard.

He was only about five-foot-six, but the big square shoulders and the mass of wavy black hair made him seem bigger, that and the way he sneered at the world down the length of his Cuban stogies. I used to know a guy on the force who would stop by every week and confiscate a couple of dozen from the runner DeLillo had hired to bring them from Canada. Never more than a couple dozen, though. More than that and DeLillo might decide it was worth getting mad about. You rarely heard again from people he got mad at.

So DeLillo had a horse in the eighth race, just like Ward. I was having a lot of suspicions confirmed tonight. As I chewed over the possibility that the two of them had just showed up in the same barn by coincidence, I looked over the yard. DeLillo was gone by now, following his horse to the harnessing area. And coming out of another barn altogether was Eli Ward. And his wife. And his son.

They were standing together like an ad for *Town and Country,* all tweed and teeth and glowing respectability. It made a pretty picture. They must have thought so, too, because after a while the kid took one of those skinny cameras out of his jacket pocket and snapped a few shots of his mother with the barns and the passing horses as background. Ward stood looking on, wincing a little every time the flash went off.

It was hard to believe that this was the lady who'd told a total stranger she was on her way to Reno, and even harder to think that I'd seen

Ward five minutes ago on the second level of a barn halfway across the yard. Apparently they were going to skip the harnessing, because they headed toward the rail, making their way past the little grandstand the management had set up for people like them and over to the edge of the paddock where you can practically lean over and touch the track. I decided to head out with them and watch the race.

Chapter 21

Not being a fashion plate has its advantages. With my dirt-gray windbreaker and my mud-brown pants, I blended right into the shadows. My visit this afternoon from the boys at Wanda's meant that somebody was already on to me, but I didn't know if that somebody was Eli Ward. For all I knew, he still thought I was Peter Hecht's uncle, and his wife and kid thought I was some creep who was worried about his niece. Besides, nobody had invited me to this family party. I slipped behind the open door of an empty stall.

Apart from a groom with a stopwatch and field glasses, the Wards had the rail to themselves. I couldn't hear what they were talking about, but at one point the doctor's hand raised from his wife's shoulder and clenched into a fist. It was just for a second, but there it was. I edged closer, keeping in the shadow of the buildings.

When the barns stopped, so did I. I was still

pretty far away, but close enough to hear most of what they were saying.

Not that it was too exciting. Ward was deep into a description of the new liniment his trainer was pushing.

"He's mixing Pearson's No. 19 Hopple Chafe Lotion with Elizabeth Arden's Eight Hour Cream and rubbing it into her legs," he was saying. "Makes the stall smell like a hairdresser's, but Mike assures me it will do wonders. And he's changing her hopples, too."

Hopples are a gizmo that go between a pacer's legs, front to back, and helps to keep the horse in balance. If Ward was expecting his family to do cartwheels over the good news, he must have been disappointed. His wife just kept on fidgeting with the strap to her purse, and his son yawned so loud even I could hear.

"Tired, Harry?" asked Ward in a sarcastic voice. "Well, that's what you get for staying out all night, young man. Don't think I don't hear you, coming in at all hours of the morning. Your mother may sit up with a glass of milk and a plate of cookies, but don't expect that kind of sympathy from me."

Maybe he was trying to sound funny and indulgent, but it didn't come out that way. Seemed to me there was a nasty edge to Ward's voice. Must have seemed that way to Harry, too, from the way he reacted.

"Why don't you just butt out of my life?" he shouted.

The groom at the other end of the rail turned to check out the noise, then went back to his field glasses.

"Slow down, young man," his father warned. "Slow down."

"Slow down!" Harry echoed. "I like that. You're the one who's at the hospital until midnight every night. Half the time you fall asleep at your office and never make it home at all! Mother's told me about the way you've been treating her lately."

Ward was patience itself. "Surely you see a difference, Harry, between working late and staying out carousing," he said in a patronizing voice. "And you know we worry about you—your mother especially. She's already decided to go out West for a rest after Easter. In the meantime, do try to have a little more consideration."

The kid let out with something that was a cross between a groan and a bellow. I couldn't blame him. If I were Ward's son, I'd have kicked the old man's teeth in for being so patient and reasonable and condescending. It's been a long time since I was seventeen, but I remember it well enough to know that the wisdom of your parents isn't much appreciated. At least Mama Ward had the sense to change the subject.

"Harry, darling," she said coolly, speaking for

the first time since I'd gotten there. "Would you please get my jacket from the barn? It's chillier out here than I had thought."

Harry darling glared at his father. "A favor from your thoughtless, inconsiderate son?" he asked mockingly. "Why not ask your devoted husband?" Then his tone shifted back to normal as he looked at his mother. "I'll be right back with it."

As he sprinted off to the stables, it became clear that the chill had more to do with feelings than with the weather.

"How dare you?" Mrs. Ward demanded shrilly as soon as he was out of sight. "How dare you tell Harry about the separation?"

"I thought it was a divorce you were talking about this time, not a separation." Ward sounded sick to death of the whole question. "Besides," he went on, "all I said was that you would be going away for a few weeks after Harrison was back at school. Surely I can say that much. You have, after all, been away before. You know how tired you always are after his visits. All that excitement, and then the reaction. He'll understand. He's not a child!"

"How would you know?" she asked scornfully. "When have you been there to watch him grow up? Always out giving your little lectures to the pretty young girls, dispensing diaphragms and prescriptions for the pill. Are you sleeping with them all, Eli?" she taunted. "Or just the ones who remind you of me?"

Ward said something I couldn't catch, but whatever it was, Helen Ward wasn't buying it.

"Why should I?" she snapped. "Why should I believe you? I know how your patients all fall in love with you. We used to joke about it, but I've known for a long time that it's no joke. You swore it was all over when Harry was born, and again when we moved to Larchmont. But those were lies, weren't they? All lies. But even if you've ruined our marriage, you can't turn my son against me." Her voice had turned into a hiss. "I'll kill you before I let you do that. I promise I will."

Ward just stood facing the track, watching them set up for the start of his race. I straightened up a bit to get the kink out of my neck. That's when I saw Harry Ward.

He was perfectly still, hunched forward a little as though he had stopped in mid-step, and too busy watching his parents to notice me. His mother had been talking pretty loud at the end, so there was no way he could have missed hearing. So much for trying to keep things from the children.

The funny thing was, he didn't seem surprised. Intent, yes, and kind of calculating, like he was figuring long odds. But not surprised. Maybe he'd seen this scene a hundred times before.

Maybe the separation was all new to him and he was in shock. Either way, he wasn't butting in. Both his folks had their backs to him, so I was the only one who saw him back off around the corner of one of the outbuildings. When he came back the second time, he was whistling. Not real loud, but loud enough to let them know he was coming. The horses were already at the gate when he helped his mother into her jacket, and he stood with his arm around her while they watched the race.

After the running they all went back to the barn. There didn't seem to be much percentage in trying to talk to Ward now. I hung around for another hour to see if DeLillo would resurface. He didn't, so I went home on the late bus, back with some of the guys I'd come out with. My ribs were starting to hurt for real, and a cold beer, a warm bed, and a heating pad sounded great.

Chatper 22

DeLillo's Suzy Q had nosed out Spots of Time to win the eighth race. Doctor's Dilemma came in a respectable fourth, which meant maybe eight percent of the purse. Thinking over those results the next morning, I decided it was time for a trip to the library.

My jaw still hurt like hell from yesterday's roughing up, and the "Today" show weatherman assured me it was going to be one of those wet, warm days that are a surer sign of spring than the red, red robin. Still, a library is a library, and I decided to shave and put on a tie.

When my father came to this country, he learned English in the Twelfth Street branch of the public library, sitting on the little chairs in the children's room and spelling out the words in the picture books. Twenty-three years old and having to ask the librarian, "What means 'fire engine'?" Back then librarians had a sense of form and the hell with feelings, and this one gave my old man two months before she told him that he was too big for the little chairs already. She pointed him to the complete works of Sir Walter Scott and told him that by the time he finished them he'd be a master of English.

I was born about halfway through. They got my name from *Quentin Durward.* Just about the earliest thing I remember is my mother cleaning up after dinner, a clatter of kids all around her in that tiny apartment, and my father sitting calm as a deaf man at the kitchen table, silently mouthing the words of the big maroon volumes with the funny engravings at the front, stopping every page or so to consult the ragged dictionary at his elbow. I don't know how many books Sir Walter Scott wrote, but my father read all of them, God rest him. When we were kids he would threaten us with the revenge of Ivanhoe or the Lord of Ravenswood if we were acting up, and during the day at the shop he would fill in all the other tailors on the adventures of the night before.

I like to think of them, immigrants all, turning out their three-piece suits for the uptown trade while they argued in broken English about the ins and outs of Scottish history. It's a wonderful place that can give you all that. I don't let anybody badmouth the library.

Yesterday's stop at Orchard Beach had beat the hell out of my sports jacket. I left it on the bedroom floor and reached way back in the closet for the top half of a gray and white seersucker suit I last wore to my sister Flora's wedding. The lapels were too thin, downright anemic-looking, but I guessed it would do.

As I bumbled around the kitchen making coffee and hunting for some paper to take notes on, I realized I was always looking back at the telephone, hoping Hecht would call. He'd stood me up the night before, but I couldn't blame him. I hadn't done the world's greatest job of finding his girl. At least he wasn't the suicide type. Some people, I'd be out right now trying to pry them off the Brooklyn Bridge. Still, I wished he'd give me a buzz. Things were beginning to add up, and I wanted to show off my arithmetic.

I had to settle for the cute girl announcer on the television. She told me all about the latest Easter bonnets and the President's plans for world peace, and I told her about how nice young girls like her had better stay away from the slimy characters that hang around the track. She finished her explanation before I got halfway into mine. But she had an easier subject.

I went downstairs and out toward the Baychester Avenue station. This was a job for the main library, Forty-second Street and Fifth Avenue. As I passed by the mail boxes, I heard a shout from the little room they have there for the so-called maintenance man. It was Sam Fuentes, already started on his daily pinochle marathon with Roger, the guy who swabs the halls when he feels like it.

"Hey, gringo," Sam yelled, waving his cards. "Hey, I got somethin' I tell you."

Sam always had something he had to tell me. Usually something about that blonde with the jackhammer legs.

"Save it for later, Sam. I'm in a hurry. Tonight you can buy me a beer on what you win from Roger." They played for half a cent a point. Big spenders.

"Hey, man, I know you. Got a hot little number just sizzling for you to put out the fire. Yeh, hey, I know. Put it to her good for me. Tonight I tell you some story. But now you go to your little *chiquita.*" Sam started pointing to his fly, and screaming in Spanish about what a hero he'd been in his day. I left him making gestures in the air like a fisherman talking about the one that got away.

The day was just as wet as they said it would be, and the subway was steaming like a jungle cruiser. Bryant Park was its usual mess of derelicts and garbage and guys peddling dope. I cut across that oasis and headed into the dry calm of the library. What I was looking for were the old newspapers. I thought it would be interesting to see how Dr. Ward's horse had been doing in general.

At the information desk they sent me down to the periodical room. There they sent me over to the microfilm room in the annex. Like everyone else, the New York Public Library has a problem with closet space, so they've stopped holding onto the old newspapers. Now they just take pictures of them and hand you a little roll of film for each month's papers. You put the film into a machine that looks like a hand-cranked victrola with a screen on top and turn the handle to get the pages rolling. Soon they'll be deciding our lives take up too much space and we'll all be on microfilm. But then who'll put us into the machines and turn the handle? I wondered if they had Sir Walter Scott on microfilm, too, or was he still in those big maroon volumes?

I was looking for two separate things, so it took a lot of trotting back and forth from the machine to the desk, trading in old rolls for new and then trading them back for the old again. I probably could have found what I wanted by checking through the back volumes of Sal Hansky's *Turf Tables,* but that's not the kind of time they keep at the library, and Lennie, my bookie, isn't so cooperative after some words we had last month. Finally, I'd got what I wanted—the Mount Vernon results for the last six years.

That was the first thing that was interesting about Dr. Ward's horse. He only raced here at Mount Vernon. Most owners take their chances at two or more tracks, maybe going up to Saratoga or at least out to Roosevelt when Mount Vernon closes down from May to July. But Doctor's Dilemma didn't show up on any of the other charts. Just Mount Vernon. He must have just kept her there, running her with a work-out boy between sessions.

The second interesting thing about Ward's horse was that he kept her at all. A nice-looking mare, but nothing to set the world on fire. She finished in the money about twenty-five, maybe thirty percent of the time, which would barely pay for her feed bill. Most guys with a horse like that, and especially most guys who only owned one horse, would get tired of waiting for her to hit her stride. They'd start putting her in claiming races, half hoping to sell her off so they could start looking around for a better prospect. In horse-racing, hope is eternal, but it feeds on fresh meat.

But Ward kept her. He kept hold of this one animal, treating her like some men treat a woman, not letting her out of his sight, not admitting that she was getting old and there were better fillies coming up. Maybe it was the horse his wife should have been jealous of, not the high school girls. Or maybe the horse was just a way to get Ward through the gate and into the barns.

While I was there, I also did some checking on Val DeLillo. DeLillo owned a lot more horses than Ward, at least four or five in his own name and probably a few more he had shares on. They ran more often than the doctor's nag and they won more often, too, but DeLillo didn't have the same sort of loyalty as Eli Ward. Just when a horse was really winning, he'd go and sell him.

The pattern seemed to be to buy up a mediocre two-year-old, turn him into a champ, and sell him at a big profit. Not a bad pattern. It just made DeLillo one of that large number of people who think *E Pluribus Unum* means Buy Cheap, Sell Dear. There was another pattern, though, that was a little more unusual. DeLillo's horses had a way of winning pretty regularly when Ward's was losing. DeLillo had trotters as well as pacers, and they won at other tracks, too, but he always won when he ran a horse at Mount Vernon against Doctor's Dilemma. And when Ward won, DeLillo never had an entry in the field.

It looked like the Sheik had known what he was talking about after all.

Chapter 23

I gave up my last reel of film and turned back to the reality of Forty-second Street. In the library, everything is always neatly filed away just where you think it's gonna be, and there's hardly anything you can't find. It's a beautiful world in there with truth and wisdom all lined up in rows, with numbers to keep everything in its place, but it's not like that on the outside.

The rain had cleared, and I stopped at the door to look at the mob scene that's Fifth Avenue at midday. Office workers, shop girls, junior executives hurrying back from lunch. Pairs of women streaming down to Lord & Taylor's or Altman's to check on the spring sales. Kids on vacation gawking around Manhattan. Plus the usual assortment of pickpockets, prostitutes, pimps, and visiting statesmen.

And who the hell knew who was who, or how to sort them out? Not me. A long-haired girl with a knapsack full of notebooks charged through the door. I dodged out of her way and left before I got trampled by any other truth-seekers.

On the street, I took off my tie and hailed the guy with the hot dog wagon. Walking east on Forty-second Street, working on my tube steak, I went over the facts again to see if they fit together the way they had in the library and out at the barns last night.

The Sheik had hinted that Ward was doping horses for the big boys, and DeLillo's results showed that Sam's nephew at least knew his rumors. Instead of getting out when he wanted, like the Sheik had said, it seemed the doc had been dragged further in, lining up girls for somebody's high-class body shop. And if the girls didn't work out, like Cissy Holder, they carved them up and chucked them out. Stuff like that must have been a big help in keeping Ward in line.

But how had they gotten to him in the first place? I got on the subway at Grand Central Station and thought about it on the long ride back to Co-op City.

For a while I didn't think I would make it. We managed to pull into the Fifty-ninth Street stop just as every woman on earth decided to leave Bloomingdale's, and I spent the next ten blocks having my right kidney massaged by a shoe box. I understand in Japan they hire pushers to jam everybody into the subway cars. Here we have Bloomingdale's customers.

At Eighty-sixth Street I decided gambling debts were a likely choice. Or maybe Ward had tried managing the girls himself and got muscled out by the pros. Maybe that was what he and Wanda had been arguing about that first night. I considered going back to Wanda, but yesterday's visit had made me wary of her kind of nursing for a while. On the way home from the station, I bought the early edition of the *Post* and a can of tuna fish for dinner.

The janitor's room was empty. Sam must have cleaned him out early and gone off to drink up his winnings. Since they've made it so you can have your welfare and Social Security checks sent straight to the bank, the mailboxes only get pried open about twice a year instead of monthly. Mine was still locked, but it didn't have anything in it worth stealing. An invitation to the Sergeants' Benevolent Association Ball, an ad for some place in the East Bronx that was enrolling now for its special low-sodium Szechuan cooking classes, and a postcard from my sister Rowena's youngest telling me how he'd hitchhiked out to Colorado to go skiing for spring vacation. The card was a picture of some crazy animal called a jackalope that looked like a rabbit with antlers. No crazier than me having a nephew who was a skier. That sport is strictly carriage trade. Imagine carrying skis on the subway.

I tucked the card in my pocket and stuffed the rest of the mail in the incinerator by the elevator.

Still no news from Hecht, but at least no threatening letters, either. Not that Wanda's buddies were the kind to write. I wondered if they even knew I'd made it back from the beach.

The phone was ringing when I got to my apartment door, the same as it had when I'd gotten started on this crummy job. I got in on the third ring.

It was the police.

Chapter 24

To be more exact, it was Abe Minelli. Abe and I started on the subway together just before the war, working the A and B trains on the Harlem line. After we both made sergeant, our routes split. Abe went for Detective and I stayed with Patrol. We still ended up working together a lot, though, even after he made captain, and we used to meet on Saturdays sometimes and go out to Staten Island to work out at his cousin's gym. The wives would bring along a lunch, we'd get a couple of packs of beer and make a picnic of it. Ten years ago, Abe's wife inherited her parents' house in Mount Vernon, and about six years ago he got an offer to run the Investigative Division of the Mount Vernon Police Department. He'd been on the Transit Authority for almost twenty years, so he took it for the change. And the promotion. We still got together once in a while, but not much after Bea got sick. The last time I'd seen Abe and Alice was at Bea's funeral.

Abe's not big on chitchat and neither am I, so

we got through the pleasantries in two sentences.

"Listen," Abe ordered. I was listening already, but that's the way he begins everything important. "Listen. We got a kid in here on suspicion of murder, and he says he knows you. Says he spends a lot of time with you." Abe sounded embarrassed. His next sentence explained why.

"I'm afraid, Quent, we have to ask you to come down here for questioning."

I was too amazed to even be mad. "What kind of bull is this, Abe?" I squawked. "Twenty-five years underground, a lot of punks get to read your name tag. This guy's probably been holding a grudge since I nabbed him for busting open a gum machine. Good grief, Abe! Who do you think I am?"

"Now hold on, Quent. Just hold on. It's not like that, see. The kid's name is Peter Hecht, and he sure knows a lot about you. And listen . . . he don't look to me like the type that knocks off a gum machine."

Peter Hecht. No wonder he hadn't met me last night. They'd probably already had him under arrest.

"Hecht, huh?" I tried to sound casual. "Yeah, I know him. Mind telling me what he's supposed to have done? Or am I supposed to know that already, being his accomplice and all?" I laid on the irony like mayonnaise. Abe didn't much like the taste.

"For crying out loud, Quent," he pleaded. "You don't think I like doing this, do you?" His voice got even glummer. "It's that girl they fished out of the Sound yesterday. Cecilia Holder. She washed up in Great Neck, but she was last seen in Mount Vernon, so they called us in. This is one too many homicides, Quent. I'm taking it myself."

"So?"

"So the Hecht kid is our strongest lead so far. Last year he knocked up the victim, then tried to drag her off to Maryland to get married. She wouldn't go—got an abortion instead—and Hecht went berserk, breaking into her house and threatening her parents and a lot of other stuff. The girl left home because he'd been threatening her, her mother says, but lately he'd found out where she was living. He'd been hanging around there a lot, these last few days. Doesn't look too good for him."

I was dumbfounded.

Abe stopped short there, then he got more businesslike. "So anyway, if you could just come on down here, you'd make everyone's life a lot easier."

Everyone but me. I got a sudden yen to visit my brother Walt in Cincinnati, but knowing Abe he probably had a couple of guys out front right now, to make sure I didn't try anything funny.

"I'll be right over, Abe," I said. "And see if you can get me some decaffeinated coffee, okay? I'm retired now. I can't drink that swill you brew for the force."

Chapter 25

I was right about the two guys outside. They offered me a ride to the main precinct, which I took. Might as well save myself the fifty cents. Twenty minutes later I stood in the doorway of Abe's office.

As soon as Abe saw me, he got up and walked around to the front of his desk, stretching out his hand and wearing that worried smile that was so familiar.

"How are you, Quent?" he asked. "How's it been going lately?"

"I thought that's what you're supposed to work out of me under the hot lights," I growled. I wasn't exactly thrilled to be there, and I wasn't feeling buddy-buddy. Especially with the police stenographer already taking everything down.

"Okay, okay." Minelli smoothed back his hair with his left hand, another gesture I remembered from way back. He was grayer now than when we'd started out, but at least he'd hung onto the hair. Some guys I know get into a habit like that and spend twenty years smoothing back their scalp.

"Listen," Abe ordered, handing me a mug and picking up one of his own. "What do you know about Peter Hecht?"

Down to business. I eased into the worn leather chair across from Abe's desk. He hadn't even apologized for the coffee. Things must look pretty bad.

What did I know about Peter Hecht? Not much, really. I put my mug down on a pile of manila folders and considered our acquaintance.

"He's a kid I met last Monday in a fast-food place over by the Raceway. We got to talking, he heard I used to be on the mole force, and he asked me to help him find his girl."

I stopped when I saw the smirk Abe was trying to hold down. "You think it's funny, huh?" I demanded. "Me getting picked up by a juvenile to run his romantic stakeout?"

Abe shrugged.

"Okay," I conceded. "So it's funny. You ever play penny-ante poker all day with a bunch of eighty-year-olds? I was bored, Abe, B-O-R-E-D. Besides, it was a joke. Nobody told me the girl was going to get killed."

But they were telling me now, and saying maybe I helped it happen. My heartburn was acting up by this time. I helped myself to the package of Tums on Abe's desk.

"You want me to keep talking, or you wanna make fun of me?"

Abe looked apologetic. "Keep talking."

So I told him what else I knew about Hecht, and about my visit to Mrs. Holder. I figured he'd know about that already, and his nod told me I was right.

"She thought you were quite a guy, Quent," Abe said. "She was real surprised you weren't from the school. I think she was looking forward to parent-teacher night." He couldn't help smiling. "Something about those big blue eyes, huh?"

"Must be," I agreed. It would be nice to dream about. "She's the one who set you after Peter Hecht?"

"She mentioned him. Then the woman the Holder girl was staying with identified his picture right away. Said he'd come around the day of the murder, insisting that he had to see Cissy Holder."

So they'd found Wanda.

"This woman didn't mention anyone else? Anyone the girl was hanging around with? Anyone who had been looking for the girl?"

"Nope." Abe was definite. "She said Hecht was the only soul who even knew Cissy Holder was there, besides her parents."

That was strange. If Wanda was so eager to throw Peter in the clink, why not me as well? Was

Abe holding out on me? Or was Wanda hoping to keep me out of it, so she wouldn't have to answer any questions about who beat me up? Going by the book, I should have told Abe about that little event, but I decided to keep it to myself. If he was going to haul me in on suspicion, the least I could do was clam up on him.

Abe motioned the stenographer to leave and swung his feet up on the desk. I noticed he was still partial to those wing-tip oxfords we all wore in the forties.

"So," he sighed. "What do you think?"

I considered for a minute, then turned to face him.

"I don't think he did it, Abe."

Abe just raised his eyebrows and smoothed back his hair, so I went on. "Maybe he did try to get the girl to marry him. He's that kind of kid. Straight. A real boy scout. But murder—what for? All he wanted was to find the girl and take care of her. What kind of a way to take care of someone is it to carve her up and dump her in the drink? I just don't see it. Did Mrs. Holder tell you he was a killer? Because from what I've seen of the lady, she'd lie her head off to make life easier without even realizing what she was doing."

Still silent. Time to take the offensive. "What about those other murders?" I demanded. "Same kind of crime, same kind of victim, same way of disposing of the bodies. You gonna tell me Hecht wanted to marry all of them? You know what *I* think?" I concluded. "I think you haven't got a case and you're trying to pin it on Hecht because he's around."

That got Abe's goat, like I knew it would.

"You know what I think?" he countered heatedly. "I think we're dealing with a schizo personality. A real Jekyll and Hyde. You say you don't see it. Well, do you see him busting into her parents' house in the middle of the night and threatening them with a gun? Or trying to abduct the girl from school? It was all hushed up when it happened, because they were both underage, but nobody's shy about talking now. And as for the bag, it's just the kind of thing an amateur would latch on to—a way to cover his tracks.

"And let me tell you something else, Mr. 'I-don't-see-it.' " Abe's eyes shifted to the scarred green wall behind me. His voice got that hard rasp of a man who's been angry so long he doesn't even know it any more. "Let me tell you a few things you may have forgotten since you've been hanging out with the prune juice set. This is the fourth case I've heard of like this since December, some nice little girl from the suburbs winding up a homicide. All these knee-jerk liberals up in Larchmont or out in Great Neck," he sneered. "They don't want to *alienate* their kids, see? So they let their little darling have a pajama party with her boyfriend, and then they wake up one morning and find out he's bludgeoned her with the Jacuzzi from her private bath. Heard about

that very case just last week. Turned out the
victim liked to pick her bedmates from the outpatient fringe of the state asylum. She figured his
shacking up with her was 'therapy.' "

Abe swung his chair down and thumped his
feet on the floor, suddenly cheerful. "I tell you,
Jacoby," he grinned, "it makes you nostalgic for
a good straight purse snatch or a stickup on the
graveyard run from Dwyer Avenue."

Abe was cheerful because he did have a case
after all, and we both knew it. Hecht had been
hanging out in Mount Vernon all Tuesday
morning. Plenty of time for him to find Cissy
doing something, somewhere, with someone that
would make him fly off the handle. Maybe he'd
called me in just to give himself an alibi. It
seemed hard to believe, but Abe had reminded me
that there was a lot about Peter Hecht I didn't
know.

But there was also a lot about Cissy Holder
that Abe didn't know. I noticed he hadn't mentioned a thing about Eli Ward, or about Cissy's
way of earning pocket money. But if he was in the
dark about that, it was fine by me. I still couldn't
get over the nerve, hauling me downtown.

Abe must have been reading my mind, because
he changed his tone again. Now he was all
friendly concern. "Where'd you get that welt on
your jaw?" he asked. "And what's with the back
of your head? You keep rubbing it like somebody
slugged you."

"Just checking to see if this office has rotted out my brains yet."

Abe was waiting for me to say something more, but I let him keep on waiting. After a while he got bored and gave up.

"Think it over, Quent," he said. Suddenly he was conciliatory. "It makes sense. Hecht is out on bail—his father came to get him this morning. If he tries to get in touch with you, let us know. And listen. If you want to come back to work, I think I can do something. We had good times, you and me."

Abe stood up. I just sat there, the original bump on the log.

"Okay, okay." Abe waved his hands in defeat. "But let me know if you get anything more from Peter Hecht. Don't make me dig it out. We go back too far for that."

Chapter 26

I walked out past the lieutenant in the front office and shut the door behind me. But I couldn't shut out the confusion in my head. The hall was empty for the moment, and I stopped to get my bearings. It was nice there, just me and the cracked linoleum and the water fountain and the hissing radiator. Then I realized it was no radiator I was hearing.

"Pssst. Over here."

I walked diagonally across the hall to where a door was open. Inide the room was Wanda Bronovitch, leaning forward in a wooden armchair, furtively waving me to come in.

Wanda. I had been itching to get my hands on that woman. And at least here she wouldn't have any goons hiding behind the kitchen door. As I stepped into the room I could hear someone talking on the telephone in an inner office.

"Sure, Inspector Minelli. I'm working on it. Oh, yeah? You think so? What else?"

Wanda interrupted my eavesdropping. "He's after you, too," she hissed urgently.

No kidding, Abe was after me. I hadn't come down here for my health. But then it turned out she didn't mean Abe at all.

"Those were Val's meatchoppers. I recognized them."

"Val? You mean Val *DeLillo?*"

So Wanda hadn't arranged that little party after all. Or at least she wanted me to believe she hadn't. But what did DeLillo want with me?

"How do you know Val DeLillo?" I whispered. "Through Ward?"

"Leave town while you're still alive."

It wasn't much of an answer, but it had an effect, I don't mind saying. Was DeLillo behind the murders?

"He just can't stand the idea that I might make some money," she moaned. "The selfish bastard. They're all against me."

The detective in the other room wouldn't be on the phone forever.

"What money? What are you talking about?" A light went on. "Is Val the one trying to pin it on the kid?"

"Him, too," she insisted. "They're all after me. And now they're after you."

The woman had a one-track mind.

"Now, just listen, Wanda. Val DeLillo killed Cissy Holder to shut down your business, is that it? What about Eli Ward? Is he in danger, too? Or is he in with DeLillo? Is DeLillo responsible for that letter you got?"

"Yes, yes," she nodded frantically, but before I could figure which question she was answering, the door to the inner office swung open.

"Hey, Miss Bronovitch. Who are you talking to?"

I ducked back out to the hall. Getting chummy with Wanda was no way to get out of the precinct house fast. Let Abe figure out who was after her. I had other fish to fry, before they fried me.

It felt like it should be tomorrow already, but the clock over the front desk said four o'clock. I waved at the sergeant on duty and sauntered out into the afternoon. As far as I could tell, there was nobody following me.

Chapter 27

My mother always used to insist that a nice bowl of soup would improve just about anything. It seemed like a good time to test her theory.

The lunch counter down the block was not the Ritz, but they were willing enough to open a can of chicken noodle. The waitress had one of those uniforms with a name embroidered over the pocket. It said Florence, in a flowing blue script.

"Hey, Flo," I asked. "Anybody ever try to kill you?"

She froze, her hand six inches off the counter, clutching a couple of packages of saltines. Then she decided I was kidding and put the crackers down next to my soup spoon.

"Sure, honey. All the time. Most after they taste my coffee. Right, Jimmy?"

The busboy shifted his bin of dirty cups to his other hip and laughed uncertainly.

"He don't speak no English," Flo confided. "His real name's Aristotle, just like the guy Mrs.

Kennedy married. But we call him Jimmy on account of Jimmy the Greek. You know?"

Another customer came in and Flo hurried over to take his order. A burly guy in a tight suit, with a ring that clanked against the counter when he put down his menu.

"Gimme a glass of milk and an outside cut of coffee cake," he ordered.

I smiled and started breaking crackers into my soup. If an ordinary lunch counter had dishwashers with assumed names and threats of violence about the coffee, why should I be surprised at anything that had happened? But it was no joke I was dealing with.

Ma was right about the soup, anyway. After I finished I felt much better. I thought about what I should do next. As far as I could tell, there were four options. I could go home and wait for Peter Hecht to call while I watched housewives from Los Gatos go crazy over winning a new washing machine on the TV quiz shows. I could go down to the steam room at the Y and try to get rid of the kinks left over from my trip to the beach yesterday. I could cash in my shares of the pension fund and start life over as a planter in Martinique.

The trouble with all these plans was, they made sense. Flushed with chicken noodle courage, I decided on the last possibility, which was to find Ward. Maybe he could explain what Wanda was talking about. Abe's theory about Peter Hecht had a kind of logic, but I just couldn't believe it. The best way—the only way—to clear Peter Hecht and get myself off the laugh list was to find out who really had had it in for Cissy Holder. Short of getting to DeLillo himself, which wouldn't be either easy or healthy, Ward was my best bet. If I could figure out for sure his connection with Cissy Holder, at least I'd have a better idea who my suspects were. I was sure Abe must be considering a few possibilities besides Hecht, but maybe I had a few express routes to the answer.

Flo was busy polishing the big blue bottle of Bromo Seltzer that hung over the glass case with the fruit in it. I put a dollar on the counter and got up to go.

"Let me know if Jimmy starts giving you long odds for the Raceway," I called in passing.

"Sure, honey. Will do." She waved cheerfully and went back to her polishing.

Chapter 28

Today was Friday, which made it Ward's day at the hospital. At least I wouldn't have to go trekking out to Larchmont. I went to the corner and waited for the bus to the Bronx River Shopping Center, over on the other side of Mount Vernon near the track.

Now let me tell you, the country that could have the bright idea of putting a hospital in a shopping center will never have socialized medicine. It was almost five when I got there. As I fought my way past the shoe stores and housewares boutiques, I was just thankful it wasn't a medical emergency. Finally, I made it to the local temple of health where Eli Ward hung out.

A gray-haired woman in a pink smock was at the information desk. She told me Dr. Ward was conducting a class in adolescent pediatrics, after which he'd be touring the floor with his interns.

"He should be through in about an hour and a half," she chirped. "Perhaps you'd like to do some shopping and come back. The stores are open until nine tonight."

I could have used a new bath mat, but I didn't want to get involved.

"I'll wait."

"As you like," she answered brightly. "The visitor's lounge is around the corner by the elevators, West Wing. Dr. Ward will be coming out that way."

After so many detours and dead ends, it was hard to believe I was actually getting close to the action. I settled down with a copy of *Sports Illustrated* to compose myself for the great confrontation.

As per usual, the racing feature was about thoroughbreds. Thoroughbreds appeal to Scotch drinkers, standardbreds appeal to beer drinkers, or at least so the thinking goes. Me, I like a bourbon on the rocks with a Dr. Pepper chaser, but I guess rags like *Sports Illustrated* bank too much on ads for Scotch to take a chance featuring trotters more than once every other blue moon.

I had gotten through a page or so on the Whitney stables' hopes for next spring's fillies when distraction came bopping out of the elevator, pushing a stainless steel cart full of dirty dishes.

It was Sam's nephew, the Sheik, looking a whole lot less devastating in a baggy hospital uniform than he had in his jumpsuit. But the

Sheik was the Sheik, no matter what he was wearing.

He made like he had been expecting me, and wheeled his cart to where I was sitting, "Hey, baby," he called. "You got my message."

"Can't say that I did," I answered. "I'm waiting for Dr. Ward to come off the floor. What was your message?"

The Sheik ignored my question. "Waiting for him to come out of the clouds, you mean," he said. "Old Ward was flying when he came in this morning." He caught my look of amazement and started to giggle. "What's the matter, gringo?" he laughed. "You think only people like me get on the juice? Maybe only people like me get busted, but whitey has been known to take a taste, I hear. And when whitey can write his own prescriptions . . ." The Sheik laughed again, and sent his cart off down the hall while he strutted along in its wake.

It was getting to be almost routine. Just when I began to think I knew what was going on, some big surprise came and sat down in front of me, blocking my way. No sense in trying to ignore it.

I checked my watch and trotted off after the Sheik. I caught up by the service elevator and got on just as the door was closing. He nodded and pressed the button for the second sub-basement.

"Was that your message?" I said. "That Ward is on the juice? What is it? Uppers? Downers? Horse?"

The Sheik's eyes widened. "Didn't you know about *that?* And here I thought you were his *amigo grande.* I s'pose I was wrong, baby. You wanna know what he takes, you ask him. All the Sheik sees are the effects." He winked and started singing a two-line calypso. "*Oh, la, la, the sweet effects. Oh, la, la, the sweet effects.*"

The elevator stopped and we got out into a corridor that looked just like the one we had left.

"No," he continued, "that wasn't why the Sheik commanded your presence. My message is from the sweet lady Wanda."

It was my turn to be surprised. "You know Wanda?"

"The Sheik knows everybody," he boasted. "Besides," he added, "I used to work out of her station when she was here on the maternity floor."

"The last time I saw Wanda I nearly got put in the clink. And the time before that I got knocked on the head for my trouble," I complained. "What does she want now?"

"That's it," he answered. "Wanda, she wants to know who you are that you have these people chasing after you to beat you up and drag you away. She was one scared senorita when I saw her last night, and that's not like Wanda at all. No way, my man."

Maybe not, but her mood hadn't changed much from last night to this afternoon. I wondered when Abe had gotten to her. It was clear the

Sheik didn't know about that. I tried to see what he did know.

"So Wanda came to you for protection?"

"Not *exactamente*," the Sheik conceded, pushing his cart through a swinging door marked Dish Room. "I saw her over at the Raceway last night. We go for some tequila and then she tell me 'bout you." He let the door swing closed and wiped his hands on his jacket. "As soon as she say the name, I know you right away. The brave lover from Tony's Cantina, eh? So I called *Tío* Fuentes, to tell you to meet me tonight. I pledged to Wanda the Sheik could find out what you're after, and that is what I want to know."

Two young men in wash uniforms pushed past us out the swinging doors.

"Hey, Washington," one of them called over his shoulder. "Break time."

"Can't you see I'm occupied with a visitor?" demanded the Sheik.

The two stopped and eyed me with open curiosity. "Carlos Washington making time with the Man," one hooted to the other. "Ain't that the living end."

They vanished down the hall. I turned to the Sheik.

"Don't worry about Wanda," I said. "She knows perfectly well what I'm after. And she also seems to know who's after me. If she's scared, it's of older friends than me—until three days ago I never laid eyes on the lady."

The Sheik eyed me cautiously. "*Tio* Sam, he told me you were a fuzz but a straight-shooter. So I s'pose you really got your nose open for that fox you told me about. Don't know why, though, gringo. Plenty other foxes in the woods, plenty cooler ones."

"I *was* looking for her," I corrected him. Apparently the Sheik wasn't keeping up with the news. "The police found her body two days ago, only they forgot to tell me about it. They think her boyfriend did it and that I helped him."

I stopped for a minute and was stupidly relieved to see the Sheik didn't buy that version. As if his opinion mattered. I went on.

"All I want now is to be able to walk in a door without wondering who's waiting for me behind it. And to pick up a newspaper without finding someone else has been knifed." I pointed to a student nurse passing by, a pretty young black girl with her hair braided close against her head. "Someone like her."

"Now, you tell me," I asked, turning back to the Sheik. "What kind of a place is it that Wanda is running? And what's her game with Eli Ward?" I thought I knew, but I wanted to hear his version.

He looked up and down the corridor, then moved closer and started talking. "Sure, I'll tell you. Why not? Wanda and the doctor, see," he confided, "they used to do the *abortos* for the girls before the Man changed the law and made it cool. First in Ward's office, then at that place in town here." He chewed his lip for a second before going on. "As for now, I don't know. Wanda split here two years ago, and when she went the Sheik moved on to other deals. We just happened to meet last night. But I hear Ward's ass is in some kind of trouble, and I mean *big* trouble. The boys got him by the short hairs." The Sheik paused. "Something to do with that horse of his, if you get my meaning, gringo."

I could hear the two orderlies joking and laughing as they came down the hall. Time for the Sheik to disappear and Carlos Washington to get back to work. "You still want the Doc?" he asked.

"Sure," I said. "Maybe he can fix me up with some other honey. But I'll be back. I've got some things to tell for your friend Wanda. When do you get off?"

"Eight o'clock," he answered glumly. "I'll look for you upstairs . . . if you're still in one piece." As I turned away, his voice brightened. "Hey, you mothers," he called to his buddies. "You didn't bring me no coffee, no Coke, no nothin'? What's with you cats?"

Chapter 29

There were at least half a dozen exits from the hospital. Most likely more. But if the woman at the information desk answered so confidently that Ward would be coming out the West Wing, he was probably a man of habit. Besides, I could only be at once place at a time, and I might as well start with the obvious one.

I had a hard time settling down. This morning at the library I had had everything figured out, but then Abe and Wanda and the Sheik had each come and handed me a tangle of new ideas I hadn't been able to sort out.

Besides, I don't like hospitals. Those last few months with Bea gave me more than my fill of sitting around waiting rooms and lounges, hoping some new doctor would arrive with a miracle. Bea's hospital was in town and this joint was new to me, but they're all alike. They all make me nervous.

Hard to say what I was nervous about, though. The worst had already happened. I only hope that when I go, I go fast. Die in my sleep of a heart attack, like my old man.

I thought some more about Bea. When you spend more than half your life with a person, it leaves a big hole when she's gone. You can try to plaster it over with busy work, or go to pieces like that guy in my building who tried to commit suicide. You can look for someone else to fill her place, which is I guess what most people do. But it's hard for me even to believe that Bea is gone. I still get up in the morning sometimes and make twice as much coffee as I need, and end up pouring her half down the kitchen sink.

To get my mind off Bea, I started checking out the rest of the people hanging around. Dinnertime was over and the place was starting to fill up. I used to have a game on the trains where I'd decide what animals different people were like. I tried it out now.

The guy by the elevator was obviously a beaver. He was practically gnawing at the woodwork, he was so eager to get upstairs. Then there was a scattering of basset hounds—sad, apologetic-looking people holding gifts that were supposed somehow to make up for the fact that they were healthy while someone else was sick. The snooty woman in the corner with her fur collar turned up was a Siamese cat—her coat was even the right color beige. I watched her reach out an expensive black boot and kick a cigarette

butt away from her part of the floor. I expected
her to start licking herself clean any second.

And all around, there were the chicks and hens.
They don't let children up on the floors, so you
always see them, worried mothers or fathers or
older sisters keeping track of a bunch of kids
while they wait for their turn upstairs.

Looking at one woman trying to keep hold of
four little ones at once, making little clucking
noises to keep them in line, I wondered if you
could classify families the same way. Bea and I
were obviously a pair of pigeons, sometimes
spitting and pecking at each other's necks, but
mostly cooing in the corners and telling each
other what a great time we were having
scratching our way around the city. But what
about the Holder family? Mama Holder wouldn't
like me to say so, but it seemed to me she was an
ostrich, hiding away from what everyone else
could see. Or maybe they were eagles—big and
powerful, but not too good at surviving in the
twentieth century.

And Ward? What about his family? I once saw
a movie about these arctic sheep, where every
year the young rams would fight the old ones for
dominance of the herd. That must be what the
Wards were like. No love lost there between
father and son.

I gave up on the animal game and thought
some more about what I was going to say to

Ward when I caught up with him. *If* I caught up with him, that was. When you thought about it, it was pretty strange the number of times I'd gone looking for him and gotten sidetracked. And each time by someone who gave me a whole new angle on the guy.

His wife hated him and his son thought he was a damn fool. Well, those views weren't too hard to find in a lot of families. But then there was Wanda, who sort of shrank up when I mentioned the name Eli Ward. And the Sheik, who made out like a guy was a slimy hophead butcher out for a buck and who could care less where it came from. And the biggest puzzler of all was how all these images fit in with the guy Peter Hecht had introduced me to at the track—the silver-haired, hearty-voiced do-gooder.

I was still chewing over this last one when the mystery man himself got off the elevator, just when the woman said he would. Ward was dressed for the street, but the young guy and the woman with him were both wearing white hospital coats. They were hanging on his words like he was Moses just back from the mountains.

They stood talking in front of the elevator another few minutes, then Ward shooed them off and made for the side door that led to the staff parking lot. I was up and waiting, and I headed him off before he had gotten six feet.

"It hasn't been easy finding you these last few

days, Doc. Either you've been real busy, or you've been avoiding me?"

I could see he remembered my face, but couldn't place it. "Hmm, let's see," he said. "Mr. O'Reilly, isn't it? You came in about some further tests for your wife." It was an announcement, not a question.

"No, Dr. Ward," I said. "It's not Mr. O'Reilly. It's just old Quentin Jacoby."

"Right," he agreed. That was nice of him. It was good to get a professional opinion that I knew my own name. He thought a second more. "You're Peter Hecht's uncle," he said triumphantly. Then he looked again. "Or are you?"

"No," I admitted. "I'm not Peter Hecht's uncle, either. You might say I'm a friend. Or you might say I'm a kind of detective. Take your pick. But pick soon, Dr. Ward. I'm tired of chasing after you while girls are getting killed all over town."

I watched his face go from polite boredom to confusion to something like fear. No sense keeping the guy in the dark.

"I started out looking for Cissy Holder," I explained. "Now I'm looking for her murderer. Don't you think it's time you stopped sneaking around and told me what happened to her? Because I think you know, and if you don't tell me," I continued, "you'll just have to tell the police."

I had said the secret word.

"Oh, my God," Ward moaned. "Cissy Holder. I saw it in the *Times* this morning." He stood still for a minute, then pulled out whatever daydream he'd fallen into. He straightened up and looked me over real carefully. For some reason I congratulated myself on getting a haircut last Thursday. Then Ward started talking, with a decision and authority I had figured must be there, but hadn't heard before.

"A detective, you say. And a friend of the Hechts. As a doctor, Mr. Jacoby, I've learned to know a person's character by what he does as well as by what he says. Now I don't know quite what it is about you, but you strike me as a person who can be relied upon. I'm taking a chance, but I think you may be the man I'm looking for."

I waited for the punch line.

"I need help, Mr. Jacoby, and I need it badly. I'm being blackmailed, and I think I'm being framed."

Chapter 30

What was this? A way to get me out the door and into some dark alley where the boys could finish off what they'd started yesterday? Was I supposed to buy that line about having an honest face? The last thing I'd come here looking for was new business. Suddenly everyone on earth was in trouble and wanted me to help. Still, here I was where all the lines intersected. Might as well talk to the man, I told myself.

"You need help?" I shrugged. "Mr. Fix-It, that's me. A good deed a day keeps the devil at bay." Then I turned serious. This lounge was not the spot to discuss blackmail. "Any place around here we can talk?"

"I'm afraid my office here isn't very private," Ward apologized. "There's a Chinese restaurant in the shopping center," he suggested. "Or we could run over to the Raceway. Frank, the head-waiter, knows me and will give us a nice quiet table in the clubhouse."

He looked around at the hospital bustle. Things

173

were already picking up for the Friday night assault on the emergency room. The lights seemed to make him nervous. Like a rabbit, I thought, wanting to return to its burrow. Or a roach trying to get back under the woodwork. Another thought crossed my mind: Or maybe like an addict getting itchy for his next fix. Well, if one of us was going to be nervous, it might as well be Ward. Like my mother used to say, just because God made you stupid doesn't mean you have to improve on his work.

"Let's stay around here," I said. "Sometimes a public place is the most private." Ward agreed uncertainly.

"You got a waiting room? A coffee shop? An employee cafeteria?" I was about to suggest a broom closet, but I didn't really want to be alone with Ward where they kept the needles.

"I know," he announced finally. "We'll go to the sun roof. Nobody will be there this time of day."

It wasn't what I had in mind. It sounded like a long and easy trip from the sun roof to the street, and Ward could be off for Larchmont while they were scraping me up with a spatula. But I decided to chance it. I motioned to the doctor to lead the way.

The sun roof turned out to be on the second floor, not on the roof at all. It was a big open room with lots of windows and no curtains, part of the corridor that connected the North and West

Wings of the hospital. The place was furnished with card tables, bright plastic chairs and some blue vinyl-covered sofas along the window wall. There was a big wooden bookcase that looked pretty well rifled, a table full of old magazines, and a black-and-white TV set pushed against the middle of the south wall. A pale young girl in a wheelchair was watching the news, but otherwise the room was as deserted as Ward had promised. He headed for a table in the corner farthest from the TV set and sat down where he could watch the traffic in the hall. I pulled a chair around next to him. If he was so hot to see the parade, it might be worth catching.

There was a long silence while we both inspected Ward's fingernails. They were very clean. Finally he started to talk, but instead of spilling out his guts he began grilling me.

"What do you know about a man named Val DeLillo?" he asked, leaning forward like a police interrogator.

"The greasy guy with the cigars and the lizard shoes?" I didn't know what Ward was after, but I decided to play along. "I know that he's a medium-sized hood who made it big in the sixties on bowling alleys and pizza joints," I began, putting together the things I'd heard from my buddy in the Racket Squad. "I know the Feds almost had him a couple of years ago on some mozzarella factory operations over in Brooklyn where the warehouses kept burning down just when the creditors were getting impatient. They never could make anything stick, though. I know he owns a big piece of the Sunshine Stables over in New Britain, and I seem to remember he's got a daughter at that college up in Poughkeepsie." I stopped to watch Ward pick at his left thumbnail. "I also know I saw you with him in the paddocks last night."

The guy almost tore his nail in half at that one, then very deliberately put his hand under the table to keep it out of trouble. As for me, I was just hitting my stride and felt like I could smell the finish. No reining in now.

"As long as you're asking, Dr. Ward," I went on, "there are some other things I know, too. Like how you've been doping Val DeLillo's horses. And taking a snort or two yourself. And then there's your little deal with Wanda—don't think I don't know about that one."

After the first shock, Ward took it pretty calmly.

"You know a good deal, Mr. Jacoby," he said evenly. "In fact, the ony way you could know all that is if you were working for DeLillo." His lips tightened. "Now, why did he send you here?"

We'd both been speaking pretty softly, but now Ward's voice got even lower and he pushed away from the table a few inches. I looked down and saw he was holding a small-caliber pistol in his lap. Pointed at me. I felt like I was going to throw up. My last living act.

Brilliant, Jacoby, just brilliant, I congratulated myself. Yesterday you pushed too hard, showing off what you knew, and you got your ribs kicked in. Nice to see how you learn from your mistakes.

I could feel the prickles of sweat all across my stomach and down my back. The girl had gone and the place was empty. I didn't see how Ward expected to shoot me point-blank in the middle of Bronx River Hospital and get away with it, but it was more than possible that he could blow me away first and worry about his mode of egress later. I started talking. My voice sounded like the other side of the world. I listened with extreme interest to what I had to say.

"Don't be crazy, Ward." Stop babbling, you jerk. I took a deep breath. "Is this the way DeLillo operates? Sending a middle-aged shlump, alone, to look you up at work? If Val DeLillo were after you, he'd have two, three of his goons waiting out at your car, and believe me, you'd be long gone by now." The lump on my head was throbbing as if to prove the point. "And if you're thinking of the police," I added, "I can tell you they don't bother with this sun roof crap either. Right now you'd be on your way to a nice cozy station house where they keep the fingerprint ink and the stenographer and the frustrated radio announcer who reads you your rights. Now you can shoot me if you want, but I don't think you want to." I sure as hell hoped not.

"No," Ward said, sliding the gun into his jacket

pocket. "I guess I don't want to shoot you." He
gave me a smile of polite apology. "I'm very
sorry, but I'm sure you can see my position. I had
to check."

The prickles were starting to go back where
they had come from. "That's okay," I choked. My
voice was trembling. I swallowed hard to get it
under control. "Is it Val DeLillo who's blackmailing you?"

Playing with the gun seemed to have set Ward
up. He didn't look half as nervous as he had
downstairs. In fact, he seemed surprised by my
question—like my appointment was over and I'd
started to tell him about some whole new disease.

"Blackmailing me?" he asked benignly, turning
to look out the window at the end of the sunset.
"On second thought, Mr. Jacoby, it's something
I'll take care of myself." He turned around to face
me, and I saw I was wrong about his voice. It was
as soft as ever, but not gentle.

"If you aren't working for DeLillo," he said
curtly, "you're working for somebody. As for me,
I've always preferred private practice."

"Bull."

Ward smiled, which got me even madder.

"I don't know who you think you're dealing
with," I said hotly, "but you don't get rid of
Quentin Jacoby that easy. First you haul me up
here in this so-called 'sun roof' at an hour when
any sensible person would be out in a nice warm

bar thinking about dinner. Then you pull a gun on me. Then you tell me to get lost. Well, I'm sorry, Doc, but it doesn't work that way. I told you I wasn't anybody's henchman, and that's the truth. I also told you I wasn't a cop, and that's the truth, too, but it doesn't mean I can't and won't go right from here to the nearest station house if you don't tell me what the hell is going on. And I don't mean about your own little problems, because frankly I could care less. I mean about Cissy Holder, who, if I may remind you, is dead. I thought doctors were supposed to care when their patients died. Or have you been spending too much time with DeLillo to let that kind of thing bother you any more?"

Ward just let me blow off steam. I finally ran out of hot air and ground to a stop.

"I'm terribly sorry, Mr. Jacoby." He said it like he had just stepped on my toe or something. "I've been under a great deal of pressure lately and I'm afraid I behaved a bit irrationally. But you see, I really don't know anything about Cissy Holder."

"Come on, Doc," I said. "I can smell bologna even when it's served up on a fancy platter. You owe me some kind of an explanation, and I aim to collect. For starters, are you being blackmailed by DeLillo—yes or no?"

"You know, I could still kill you. Temporary insanity. The pressures of overwork. I was reading about it in the *Journal of Forensic Medicine* just this morning. They'd never convict me."

"Come on," I repeated.

Ward fell back to examining his nails. He sighed. "Yes," he murmured. "Val DeLillo is blackmailing me."

"What's he got on you?"

Ward just sat there poking his cuticle like a damn manicurist, so I filled in the story for him.

"You're on junk and he knows it, but he'll keep quiet in return for professional favors, right? DeLillo's horses have been coming in pretty often lately, and the grapevine says you're helping that happen. Any truth to that?"

Ward just nodded. A real talkative type.

"Have you thought of going to the police?" I asked. "Whatever you've done that DeLillo's got on you, the authorities will overlook a lot if you help them get the goods on that two-bit mobster. And he doesn't have to know it was you who put him away. Believe me, Ward, it'll work."

"No, it won't." The words seemed to have been hanging in the air, a big pin just waiting to puncture my balloon.

"Why not?"

"Because if anything like that happens to DeLillo, he'll know it was me," Ward explained impatiently. "He's not a stupid man, Mr. Jacoby, whatever else he may be. And even if I could arrange matters with the police, I'd never be able to practice medicine again. They'd take away my license. Even if you've kicked the drugs, they suspend your license, and with the horses thrown in . . ." His voice trailed off into despair, then picked up again. "Whatever else he did, DeLillo would make sure my name hit the papers, and I think you'll agree that wouldn't do a great deal for my practice. On the other hand, I don't find much appeal in the idea of changing my name and moving to Nebraska, starting over again as an unknown GP at my age. So you see, Mr. Jacoby, I'm in something of a bind."

He smiled bitterly. It was dark now, and you could see the illuminated snake of the highway out beyond the parking lot. The corridor was filling up with the clatter of dinner trays being taken away. A passing orderly turned on the lights in the sun roof. There were all the signals that our conversation was over, except that as far as I was concerned it hadn't really gotten started.

I decided to go back to the beginning, to Cissy Holder and the house on Eurydice Avenue.

Chapter 31

First, though, I tried to find out more about DeLillo's setup.

"You say Val DeLillo is blackmailing you into doping his horses. You do any jobs for him outside Mount Vernon?"

Ward shook his head. "I suppose I should be thankful for that," he said with heavy irony. "At least he doesn't make me travel the circuit. When I first got Doctor's Dilemma, I took her over to Roosevelt for a couple of seasons, and once even down to Florida. But since I've gotten involved in the medical end of racing, the thrill of ownership has rather dwindled. Now I just keep her at the stables down the road there, and that's the only track I visit."

"And DeLillo has never pressured you to work anywhere else?"

Ward shook his head again, looking even more tired than before.

"So who does his doping for him at the other tracks?" I persisted. "Sunshine Stables has a lot of horses, and a lot of them finish in the money these days. Somebody must be taking care of the rest of the circuit."

"Perhaps," Ward agreed. "Though I'm not sure. Our acquaintance is rather unusual. And what I do takes a certain amount of skill to go undetected. Perhaps DeLillo's other horses just win on their own. That does happen sometimes, you know."

"Sometimes." I edged closer to the main issue, picking my words. "Is DeLillo also taking a cut from the crib on Eurydice Avenue?"

Ward looked up sharply. "How did you know about that?" he asked, genuine surprise in his voice. "I haven't been over to Eurydice Avenue in years."

It was my turn to be surprised.

"Let me get this straight, Doc. Are you telling me that you don't have anything to do with that little dormitory of Wanda's over by the Raceway? And that you don't know that girls with problems, girls like Cissy Holder who come to you for help, are getting trained for the streets there to support their habits? Are you telling me that, Dr. Ward?" I stopped before the contempt in my voice got too loud for the family groups that were beginning to gather at the other tables.

Ward sat staring glassy-eyed across the room. I looked out with him. An old lady came in, leaning on two canes and held up by a middle-aged man who looked to be her son. A nurse trotted down the corridor swinging an armful of charts. Worried visitors brushed past each other, rushing from wing to wing before disease and death cheated them of their friends and relatives. Ward stared at them all, but whatever he was seeing was inside.

"So that's what she's up to," he groaned finally. "And I referred the Holder girl to her, as a sentimental gesture." He gave one more glance out into the room and then shifted around the table so his back was to the crowd. He was going to talk, and he'd just have to trust his luck that all the others there were too tied up in their own misery to care about his.

"I don't know how you know so much about Wanda," he began, "except that you seem to know about everything. But let me tell you about her from my side." He settled into his chair. He suddenly looked old, like all his bones had sagged.

"Miss Bronovitch and I met about ten years ago. And when we met, that was all she was to me —Miss Bronovitch. We were working together on a youth counseling program they had here at the hospital, when there was still federal money for that kind of thing. It was clear a lot of the girls we saw were going to look for back-alley abortions. The legalization bill seemed stalled forever in the state legislature, and finally Wanda and I felt we had to do something ourselves to keep some of these girls from ruining their lives."

He paused to check my reaction. I didn't pass.

"Don't think I'm some sleazy opportunist, Jacoby," he bristled. "I did what I felt I had to do as a man of conscience. You can't understand it until you've seen a sixteen-year-old who's bleeding to death after trying to fix herself up with a knitting needle, or had to tell a bride she'll never have children because of the job some butcher did on her ten years ago." He straightened up, swollen with indignation. "These girls have a right to life, too."

"And Wanda?" I asked. I wanted to get back to her.

"Let's just say that Wanda can be very sympathetic if she wants to. She had a wonderful way with the girls in the recovery room, and she used to get quite exercised over how none of this would be necessary if parents showed their kids some affection. You know, that's the main reason a lot of these girls get pregnant. They think of a baby as some kind of an adorable machine with hot and cold running love that will make up for all they're missing everywhere else. And then when they realize they can't handle it, they come looking for an abortion.

"Anyway, one thing led to another. Wanda's changed a lot but she was still a lovely young woman then, and she looked up to me like I was some kind of god." He grimaced. "Things weren't too happy at home, and before I knew it, I was having an affair with my surgical assistant. It lasted five years, but it's over now and has been for a long time."

"Does your wife know about Wanda?" I asked. "Is that why she's leaving you?"

"Helen?" He said the name as though he had almost forgotten she existed. "Helen is a very possessive woman." He interrupted himself as he realized where he'd been drifting. "I take it you've met my wife along with everyone else in my life," he observed sharply. "May I ask where?"

"Sure," I answered. "That's easy. At your house. I went out there to see you on Wednesday, but you weren't home. Your wife's a very good-looking woman," I added. Just to show I really had been there.

"Handsome is the word that's generally used. Some people cite her classic features." His voice softened, as though he were talking to himself. "Strange, isn't it, how she held up through the drugs, through the clinic, through Wanda. But now that I'm trying to get out of the hole and put things back together, she turns around and decides she can't take it. I suppose she's been telling you all about it. Complaining seems to be her newest hobby. She and my son spend hours together talking about what a brute I am."

The wife was a mistake. We were getting further and further from where I wanted to be, which was back to Eurydice Avenue.

"If it's all over with you and Wanda," I asked, "how come I saw you two so chummy over at the Raceway Tuesday night?"

"Good God, Jacoby!" he exclaimed. "You really have been everywhere. Were you spying on me all that time before you showed up with the Hecht boy? But since you're such an expert on all phases of my life," he continued, "you must know that that was the first time in months—since last November, in fact—that I'd seen Wanda. She called me at the office and said she had to talk right away. We met for dinner at the clubhouse.

"Helen was furious when I said I wouldn't be home. We had tickets for the opera, *Lucia di Lammermoor*, and Harry was tied up with some debutante party. Helen had to go alone. She was already back when I got home from the Raceway. Sitting in the kitchen in her bathrobe in the dark—a favorite occupation of hers these days. She wouldn't even speak to me.

"Actually," he mused, "when Wanda and I got together last November, it had been at least a year and a half since I had seen her. I was appalled by how she'd toughened up, though I guess I should have seen it coming. It doesn't matter why we parted, but I don't mind telling you that Wanda has powers of persuasion that made me get over the conviction that I never wanted to lay eyes on her again. That first time, last fall, she presented me with what she termed a business proposition. I should renew the lease on the house on Eurydice Avenue and also apply for a license for the place as a bona fide abortion clinic. Then she would run it. There's a lot of money to be made out of those clinics, you know, especially if you don't mind bilking the state. Wanda didn't mind.

"I told her I wasn't interested, and I thought that was the end of it. Then she called again last Tuesday. All through dinner she kept telling me how she had to get out of town. Her big plan was for us to run away together and set up a clinic upstate." He smiled and made a show of patting his heart. "Romantic, isn't it? When I reminded her I had a wife and son, she started to get tough. When I first stopped seeing Wanda, she made some pretty ugly scenes, including a few nasty phone calls to my home. It made for a rather strained atmosphere in the family, and she threatened to start that again. Even with the threats, though, she seemed more desperate than angry. I had the sense she needed to have her scheme work out. Then she accused me of being in league with DeLillo, of wanting to murder her, of all kinds of crazy things. I tried to reason with her, but she kept on raving about how she was next. I couldn't make head or tail of what she was talking about. Of course, that was before Cissy Holder's death. The other girls—well, it still seemed like some kind of horrible coincidence."

Ward stopped and turned speculative. "Do you suppose DeLillo really is out to get Wanda?" he asked. "I'd have thought they'd be partners, not rivals, but I don't always understand these things."

I ignored the question and asked one of my own. "What does Wanda have to do with Val DeLillo?"

"You mean there's actually something you don't know?" he asked mockingly. "As it happens, she's his sister."

You could have knocked me over with a horse-fly. After a second, I found my voice.

"With a name like Bronovitch?"

Ward smiled at my amazement. "She calls herself 'Miss,'" he explained, "but that's her married name." My jaw was still flapping on my collarbone, so he went on.

"Wanda's father died so long ago she doesn't even remember him. Mrs. DeLillo was Polish, and when Wanda was seventeen her mother married her off to a nice Polish contractor named Stefan Bronovitch—an older fellow, and, I suppose, in her eyes quite a catch. They had a huge wedding over at St. Stanislaus Cathedral, in the Bronx. Wanda told me all about it one night. Poured her heart out. I thought she'd never stop crying."

Ward got lost in a romantic reverie. I called him back.

"What happened to the hubby?"

Ward looked up, remembered where he was, and started talking again.

"On her wedding night Wanda assumed her

new husband was drunk, but by the third day of the honeymoon, even one of her tender years could figure out he just wasn't the kind that went for girls. I suppose it helped clarify matters when she found him in bed with one of the bellhops.

"Lord knows what was on his mind when he married Wanda. He seemed to have done it as the respectable thing to do, without really thinking about what would happen later. Anyway, Wanda agreed not to put Bronovitch through the humiliation of an annulment if he would stake her to nursing school and never see her again. As far as I know, they're still legally married. If Bronovitch is still alive. The funny thing is, I don't think her mother ever found out."

Ward was getting caught up in Wanda's story. I guess he liked it better than his own. I was getting interested myself, so I let him continue.

"Mrs. DeLillo had cancer of the pelvis. That was why she was so eager to get her baby daughter married and settled in life. Wanda knew she was sick and didn't want to upset her, so she somehow made it seem that everything was fine. Not that she had to keep it up for long. Her mother died about three months after the wedding—of a heart attack, as it turned out. That's when Wanda started nursing school, with tuition paid by Bronovitch. Pizza was just starting to catch on then, and Val wanted to get into the business. First he threatened to kill Bronovitch for double-crossing his sister, but

then he settled for a 'loan' to set himself up. Soon
he started supplying cheese to all the pizzerias
around. He evidently had a very effective sales
force."

I nodded. I had gotten the hard sell and free
delivery to Orchard Beach.

I was beginning to understand that funny
combination of nice-girl-gone-tough that was
called Wanda Bronovitch, but that didn't make
me like her any better or trust her any more. I
asked Ward when he found out all this stuff
about DeLillo.

"About the same time he found I was taking a
few too many barbiturates. My wife had taken
Harry to visit her parents in Palm Springs, and
Wanda and I were up at Val's farm in Connecti-
cut, near Litchfield. A lovely place—beautiful
colonial house, and his own stable and practice
track. While we were there, I ran out of pills. Val
very considerately offered me some of his private
bond cocaine. The perfect host, you might say.
Besides, it was a pretty high-living crowd that
weekend. After that he came over with little gift
packages every so often. A number of my
colleagues think cocaine isn't addictive, but let
me tell you, you can get quite dependent on that
stuff. I was pretty far gone before it turned out
that it wasn't a gift at all. When Val DeLillo
sends you a bill, it's a big one."

"You mean he actually charged you for it?"

"No, of course not." Ward waved away the suggestion. "He just made it very clear that as long as I was getting so pepped up, it would be nice if his horses could, too. That was the exact phrase he used—'so pepped up.' I remember it well."

Things were starting to fall together again, but in a different pattern than before. Through the window I could see the lights of the clock on the Bronx River Savings Bank. Twenty to eight. I didn't have much time.

"Listen, Dr. Ward," I said brusquely. "I can't wait for explanations, but I think I can help you get DeLillo off your back. Just try to sit tight for another day or so. The police will probably be on to you soon, especially if you still hold the lease on the place where Cissy Holder was hiding out. Don't make up any stories, but don't volunteer anything, either. Say you're waiting to talk to your lawyer. One last question. You said you were being framed. For what?"

I now know how the straw felt when it broke the camel's back. Talking about Wanda had let Ward forget some of his own problems, but they came back now. He let out a sigh you could sail a boat with.

"I wasn't sure at first," he groaned. "Last week I got a letter pushed under my front door. A crude thing, pasted together from words cut out of the newspaper, full of vague hints that the writer knew what I was up to and wasn't going to let me get away with it."

So Ward was on the same mailing list as

Wanda. At least that meant he wasn't sending the things.

"At first I dismissed it as the work of a child, or a crank," he said. "Some of my patients aren't too stable. Since this morning, I've been afraid there's something more."

"What happened this morning?"

Ward drummed his fingers on the table. "I went down to the water before breakfast. I go every morning to feed the swans. This morning I found a woman's dress outside my boathouse, covered with blood. It had the same kind of pasted-together note on it. All it said was, 'Try to explain this when the police come.'"

Chapter 32

If Ward wasn't sending the letters, who was? Val DeLillo had his hook into both his sister and Eli Ward, but he wasn't the type who went in for threatening letters. Too subtle. Much as I hated to, I remembered Abe Minelli's theory about Peter Hecht, if only because it was such a damn-kid kind of stunt. And Peter had plenty of reasons to be mad at both Wanda and Ward, after the way they'd been taking care of his girl. But was he mad enough to be driven to murder? Somehow I had a feeling that dress once belonged to Cissy Holder. Ward's dock would be as good a place as any if you were out to launch a dead body, and Peter Hecht knew all about Ward's dock. Of course, so did a lot of other people, including Eli Ward himself.

"Do you have the note here?" I asked. I expected him to say he had destroyed it, or put it in the family safe, but he silently pulled a plain envelope from the inside pocket of his jacket. Sure enough, the note was the same kind as the one Wanda had shown me. The lady was right to be scared.

"Any idea where this came from?"

Ward had gone back to studying his fingernails. "Not really," he said finally. "I'm embarrassed to admit that at first I thought it might have been my son, Harry. Before I knew about the Holder girl, that is. I thought the notes might be his idea of a joke. We haven't been getting on any too well lately. Helen had a very difficult time when Harry was born, and she's never really recovered—the emotional strain. It's not his fault, of course, but the boy has always felt guilty, somehow—responsible. Lately, though, he seems to have transferred his guilt to me, and now I'm the villain. A typical rebellion against the father, and a necessary part of establishing one's own identity, of course . . . but not entirely a pleasant process if you happen to be the parent whose influence must be overcome. Nor do I appreciate the way my wife has been egging Harry on. The consolidation of ego may be necessary, but it doesn't have to be quite so brutal as this."

I couldn't understand half of his gobbledygook, but I guess I got the drift. "Brutal enough for murder?" I asked.

It was a hard question to ask a man about his son, but Ward didn't even seem bothered.

"Absolutely not," he said with finality. "Harry is the last person on earth I would deem capable of such a thing. I think you rather misunderstood what I said about adolescent rebellion. I'm *glad* Harry is starting to break away from his family. It's time he did so. Such rebellion is a healthy sign of normal development. It does not lead to a life of crime. Next you'll be suggesting it was my wife who murdered Cissy Holder."

"Okay. Did your wife murder Cissy Holder?"

Ward gave out a sound that was more a bark than a laugh. "Ah, well," he said with a grimace. "I suppose I asked for that. But, no, my wife did not kill the girl. Not that Helen is incapable of passion, because she isn't—I've had a fair amount directed at me lately," he said ruefully. "Even violence, I suppose. But leaving aside the whole question of motive, let's just say that Helen lacks the, er, temperament necessary to carry out so complex a crime. I find it impossible to think of her as a criminal mastermind. Helen is the sort of person who faints in the dentist's chair. When the cat brings in a dead bird, she just stands there and screams until Harry or I clear it away. In the extremely unlikely event that Helen were ever to commit murder, there would be no question of her guilt. She would probably stand in catatonic shock next to the body, waiting for the police to make it disappear."

He laughed briefly at his own image, then went on. "Helen's a very dependent woman," he said. "I suppose that's what attracted me to Wanda—her strength."

Suddenly he turned to face me. "Of course," he said abruptly, wonderingly. "It's Wanda. It's Wanda who's been sending those letters." His voice got stronger as he began to build his case. "She's trying to pressure me into helping her out. And she's not above violence, if it comes to that. Cissy Holder was staying with Wanda. Rochelle Bellini was another patient I referred to her. And that other poor girl—I don't know who she was, but they found her practically on Wanda's doorstep, didn't they? It has to be Wanda," he concluded positively.

"Maybe," I conceded. "But more likely not." I could have told him about Wanda's own letters, but there was another angle I wanted to explore. "For example," I asked, "how do I know you didn't kill Cissy Holder and then just plant that dress with the note to throw suspicion away from yourself? You were ready to kill me not long ago. Or was that just a little playful fooling around?"

Ward looked wary, but at least he didn't use the hint to try the gun on me again. "Why would I kill Cissy Holder?" he demanded.

"You tell me. Maybe because she knew too much about you and Wanda. Maybe she knew about you and the horses. You told me yourself how you'd be ruined if that ever got out."

"No, Jacoby, no," Ward insisted. "No, you've got it all wrong. I didn't kill Cissy Holder. I'm a doctor. I save lives. Think about it, Jacoby. Think about those other girls."

"I have been thinking of them. You know, I couldn't help noticing the other day that your wife doesn't think you're the most faithful guy around. It is possible that there's maybe some truth in her suspicions? After Wanda stopped being such a sweet young thing, did you just go home to your wife, or did you maybe start making time with some of your patients? The ones who looked up to you like you were some kind of god? But Wanda had shown you how hard it was to end an affair without complications, so maybe it just seemed more convenient to make sure things were really over when you wanted them to be. You know what I mean?"

Ward just sat back and looked at me, stunned. "Do you really believe that?" he asked softly.

I shrugged. "It's a possibility." I pushed away from the table and stood up. "Stay home tonight. I might want to reach you."

Ward nodded dumbly, but made no move to go. I left him watching the time-temperature sign on the bank outside the window. Fifty-three degrees at 8:02. I was late.

Chapter 33

The elevator took forever, but the Sheik was still waiting when I got downstairs. The white hospital coat had been exchanged for a dark red crushed-velvet suit with snakeskin trim around the pockets and lapels. One kind of uniform for another.

"*Buenas noches,* gringo," he sang out when he saw me. "I was afraid your little huddle with Dr. Ward had you hung up, but here is your honky self."

Behind the banter he was eyeing me cautiously. No wonder. One of the things that had been echoing in my mind for the last hour was the way Ward had turned on me when I told him I knew about the drugs and the horses. The doctor was right. There was no way I could have known about that except from DeLillo, and the fact that I was getting my info from the Sheik only meant there was a middleman the doctor wasn't aware of. It was hard to think of Sam Fuentes's beloved nephew as one of Val DeLillo's boys, but I didn't see any other option. The question was, should I string him along or let him have it? The emergency room was a comforting twenty feet away. Might as well let him have it.

"Here I am, all right," I agreed. "And while I was gone, I began to wonder about a few facts. Like that cock-and-bull story about meeting Wanda at the Raceway. Did DeLillo make that up for you, or was it all your own invention?"

I could see his hand tighten around the hat brim. "What I speak is truth, gringo," he insisted. "The Sheik knows what the Sheik knows." I was getting good and tired of hearing him talk about himself that way. "The Sheik knows what the Sheik knows," he repeated. "I don't run with killers like DeLillo."

"Better you should say Val DeLillo doesn't run with dirt-brown punks like you, Carlos," I snapped. "What did you offer to get him to take you on? My skin? Or a fifty percent commission on your sister?"

That brought out the Latin side, all right. Before I could blink, he was out of his chair and twisting my left arm behind my back. Hard.

"Time to leave here, baby. Pronto." He squeezed the words out from behind clenched teeth. "I don't work for Val DeLillo, but you keep jawing like that and you're going to wish I did."

We edged over to the parking lot exit, me doing that jerky hop-step I'd made so many perpetrators do when I'd collared them and marched them out to be booked. I didn't like it one bit being on the other end of the treatment, but the Sheik had a good thirty years on me and was probably packing a knife. I had no intention of ending my days as a headline.

I liked it even less when we got outside. It was dark out there, and the parking lot reminded me of the one where I'd been dumped at Orchard Beach. The highway and the airplanes and the ambulances provided background music, but it still seemed uncomfortably quiet. Where were all the shoppers when I needed them? I started talking.

"You see, Carlos, I'm on to you." I managed to sound calm and even a little amused. "Ward wasn't flying or anywhere near it. And if it's such common knowledge that he's fixing DeLillo's horses, he'd have been barred from the track long ago. And in jail. The only way you could know that stuff is if DeLillo told you, and the only reason he'd tell you is to get the word around and ruin Ward. 'Cause one thing you've got is a big mouth. But what I still don't figure is, why? Why does DeLillo want to put the jinx on his own racket? Just tell me that and I'll go home happy."

For an answer the Sheik tightened his grip on my arm and shoved me faster across the lot.

"You want to know why, gringo, you just ask Wanda. She's running the show, and make no mistake about it."

"That's very interesting," I panted. My arm

felt like it was developing a second elbow. "Was it you Wanda called from the nursing home yesterday? And don't give me that bull about her having nothing to do with that little welcoming committee."

We were passing under an arc light, and I could see the Sheik's teeth flash in a sudden grin. "Some boys, aren't they?" he giggled. "But no soul," he added disapprovingly. "No machismo." I was glad to see we agreed on something.

"Sure it was me she called. How many friends she got? But don't look to me for your hurts, man. I told Wanda Val would send over his boys if she went back to that crib, but does she listen to me? Oh, no. She's *la primera* expert and I'm just the nigger orderly to her. Good enough for keeping the girls happy, though," he chuckled.

The Sheik slowed down as he got closer to his own affairs, which was just fine with me. Something new had come up, and I wanted to be able to concentrate without worrying if my arm was going to fall off.

"So you're working with Wanda, not DeLillo," I mused. "And that was all nonsense about just happening to meet her out at the Raceway. I was wondering how come a big spender like DeLillo was letting you waste your time emptying bedpans. All I could figure was he was grooming you to muck out the horses' stalls. But Wanda—now there's a dame who's strictly low rent."

"Jacoby, baby," the Sheik said, "you're one

dumb honky fool." Still keeping his grip on my arm, he flashed his other hand to his hatband. Suddenly I was looking at four inches of cold blade.

"I don't want to cut you, man," he said reluctantly. "But if it takes cutting to keep you out of the way, cutting there will be. This is my chance to get a piece of the action, and no over-the-hill fuzz is going to get in my way. You should have stayed home drinking beer with *Tio* Sam. That's where you belong, old man."

We must have made an interesting picture there in the parking lot. It seemed like we stood there for a decade or two, the Sheik looking at me and me looking at the knife poised in front of my Adam's apple. We probably would have stayed there for a decade or two longer if the sedan in front of us hadn't suddenly come to life. The second the lights came on, the Sheik vanished. I could hear someone pounding after him across the lot.

"Having a little trouble, Quent?"

It was Abe Minelli. As my eyes adjusted to the headlights I saw other figures moving around the parking lot. One of them had already exchanged the Sheik's knife for a pair of handcuffs.

"Christ, Abe, have you been tailing me all day?" I didn't know whether to be overjoyed or insulted.

"Who cares about you?" Abe said bluntly. "You're just lucky we were around. We're

waiting for a certain Dr. Ward to come out—
that's his car you're leaning on. Seems he treated
the Holder girl and also those two others who got
killed last week. Some coincidence, eh?"

So Abe wasn't completely in the dark about
Ward after all. At least I'd gotten to him first.

"Who's your friend with the knife?" Abe asked
absently, peering over my shoulder to make sure
he didn't miss anything while we were talking.

"A little boy trying to be a big man," I
answered. "I'll tell you all about him. And don't
worry about Ward," I added. "If you miss him
here, you'll find him at home inside an hour." I
waited to give Abe a chance to be impressed. He
just raised his eyebrows, but that was enough. I
took the plunge.

"Right now, Abe, I think it's time you and I
joined forces. Or am I still a suspect?"

They had turned off the headlights, and it was
so dark I could barely see Abe smoothing back
his hair. "Of course you're still a suspect," he said
finally. "Everybody's still a suspect until we find
out who did it. You know that.

"But that doesn't mean we can't talk," he
added cheerily.

Chapter 34

Abe left his lieutenant to wait for Ward, and in fifteen minutes the rest of us were back at Mount Vernon headquarters. My hope was that maybe the hot lights would persuade the Sheik to flip for us, and I wasn't disappointed. It turned out Sam's nephew had a clean record, and Abe hinted he might keep it that way by talking. The Sheik began with what was closest to his own concerns.

"It's just a simple way to make some beautiful bread, my man. You sell what they want to buy. Manna from heaven. *Dinero* for what should be *libre!*"

"Hah," Abe snorted.

"Wanda and me, we're gonna be business partners. We operate on her hustle. She don't dig her brother, see. He's one rich *hombre,* but he's cold with his cash and won't give any to his blood. And you know why not?"

We didn't, but the Sheik was willing to answer his own question. He was moving off the defensive and starting to enjoy himself. The truth was his last tool of power.

"Because he found out her and Ward had been fixin' up the *chiquitas*, doing abortions, that's why. And that, amigos, is the truth. He telephoned once when I was there, long time ago, and I could hear him screaming into the horn how it was an act against the Savior and a disgrace to his mother's name. Like that. Crazy gringo fool," he added contemptuously.

"What else?" I prodded.

"So Wanda, see, she decides to burn him back right in his dago pride, and make a little bread for herself. Being a nurse, my friend—you *know* you don't get rich at that job. So Wanda started training some foxes of her own for the customers. A little competition to make her brother's friends mad at him, you know?"

Carlos was really catching his stride. With Abe hanging on every word, he was the Sheik again. He smoothed the nap on his jacket and went on.

"Wanda, she got tired of dealing with all these stupid little spoiled chickies. She told me that. So she goes to Dr. Ward and begs him to come back to her and start a real abortion hustle. When he didn't buy that, she got mad for real and told her big brother how she was going to turn them both in to the Man for juicing the horses."

Abe looked up questioningly.

"Sure," the Sheik asserted. "Ward, he been

fixing DeLillo's horses for two, three years. He is known far and wide as the *ultimo* horse doctor."

"You got any proof?"

The Sheik shrugged. Abe lost interest. "Let's get back to these murders on Eurydice Avenue," he ordered.

The Sheik nodded significantly in my direction. "That's when DeLillo sent some *hombres* to teach Wanda a lesson. After she started threatening him. Except they got confused, my friend, and did their number on you instead. Thought you were her partner. Poor old man," he said, shaking his head in mock dismay.

I pulled in my gut and promised myself I'd practice some karate on the twerp as soon as we were both out in the open. At least now I knew exactly why I had been beaten up. Meanwhile, Abe was getting impatient.

"Listen," he barked. "This is all very nice. A real lovey-dovey family. But what has it got to do with the Holder girl?"

"I can answer that," I said. "Cissy Holder was one of Wanda's fillies—I don't suppose her mother told you about that. After she left the convalescent home where Wanda was working she went to stay at the house on Eurydice Avenue instead of going home. Ward used to refer girls to the convalescent home, but I don't think he really knew about the other setup."

Abe looked skeptical. "Cissy Holder was the

second girl in three days murdered from that
street, and the third in the area in a week," he
whispered. "And you're telling me Ward knew
from nothing?" He turned back to young
Washington. "Was that all part of Val DeLillo
getting rough?" he asked.

The Sheik shook his head helplessly. "That,
man, is what I want to know."

"The name's Inspector Minelli. Make sure you
don't forget it." Abe turned to me. "You had any
dinner? I'm going to call out for sandwiches."

It was past ten, and for the last two hours I'd
been dreaming of the Friday night special at
Howard Johnson's. Fried clams. Too late for that
now. I settled for a roast beef club and a side of
potato salad. While the lieutenant was dialing the
order, I filled Abe in on some of Wanda's other
plans.

"Whatever DeLillo was doing," I said, "it made
a big impression on his sister. She was planning
to leave town any day now, probably for some
place upstate. She tell you that?"

She sure hadn't bothered to tell the Sheik.
While the lieutenant talked to the sandwich man,
the Sheik told the world in pretty graphic terms
just what he thought of his would-be business
partner. If the guy on the other end thought we
were ordering cheap bitch on toast, I couldn't
blame him. I never got to find out, though,
because just then a tall, red-headed officer came
in with a list of messages as long as your arm.

"Lieutenant Rodriguez called," he began in a kind of singsong that suggested there was lots to come. "He escorted Dr. Ward to his home and is going to question him there, if that's all right. And Lieutenant Gleason wants to know what to do with Miss Bronovitch. She flat out refuses to go home. Says she demands police protection, but won't say why.

"By the way," he added, "she doesn't live in Mount Vernon at all. She's just camping out in that place on Eurydice Avenue where we questioned her the other night. Wearing a friend's clothes. The whole bit. She says she has an apartment in Bronxville, but she's been too scared to go there for the last week. Now she refuses to go back to Eurydice Avenue, either. Won't touch the place where she works. Won't tell us what she's scared of. Won't tell us anything. Just says they're out to get her. Gleason said I should ask you what to do with her. Also Captain Erikson wants to talk to you about that embezzlement case. Also your wife called."

Abe sighed and looked at his watch. "Tell Rodriguez to go ahead, but remind him to make sure Ward doesn't go anywhere when he's through with him. I'll see Gleason and the lady in my office in five minutes. I've got some new information that may loosen her up enough so we can figure out what she's talking about. And call Al's Deli and tell him to forget the roast beef club." Abe turned to me apologetically. "Al's service is godawful slow at night. Might as well go home and get some sleep. Nothing happening tonight. I'll talk to you in the morning."

I started to argue, then decided that going home wasn't a bad idea. The Sheik had been looking around for a way out ever since he had heard they had Wanda. Now he sprang up from his chair and made for the door, but Abe pushed him back.

"You, pal, are staying right here." Big Red had returned by this time. "Book him on assault with a dangerous weapon," Abe ordered over his shoulder as he headed out the door. "The gent tried to cut my former colleague Quentin Jacoby."

Chapter 35

There are moments when a man begins to question his deepest principles. This was one of them. For the first time in my life, I wished I had a car. There was no way I was going to get home before tomorrow if I waited for the bus. Finally, I did the unthinkable and flagged down a cab. And talk about inflation—it's a good thing I'd missed out on those fried clams. As it was, the cabbie wasn't too happy with his tip. I thought about Peter Hecht and his grandmother's money. It had been a nice dream while it lasted. But I reminded myself that I was in this for my own satisfaction now, and that's something you never get without paying.

The first thing I did when I got home was open the can of tuna lying on the kitchen counter. The second was call Abe. There was something important I'd forgotten to ask him.

While I waited for the switchboard to find him, I picked at the tuna with my fingers. Finally there was some action on the other end of the line.

"Minelli here."

"Evening, Abe." I wiped my hands, leaving oily streaks on the dish towel. "It's me. Quentin. You getting anything from Wanda?"

"Nah," Abe sighed disgustedly. "This dame has constipation of the mind. And that Washington kid doesn't know much either. You think that stuff was true that he was feeding us about Wanda and her brother?"

"Sure. Who could make up anything that stupid? And let me tell you, somebody sure stomped on me yesterday, and it wasn't the Easter Bunny. That's not why I called, though."

"So, why *did* you call?" It was after midnight, and Abe didn't sound too interested. But at least he was listening.

"Did you ever find out for sure when the Holder girl was killed?"

Abe's voice brightened. "Yeah, we did—a real lucky break. It turned out she'd picked up a pizza from a place down the block at 6 P.M. Tuesday, and had time to eat it, too. The lab doctors put her death sometime between 7 and 11 P.M."

Hell of a final meal, I thought. I thanked Abe and told him to give my love to Alice. After I hung up, I thought about who'd been where Tuesday night. Peter had been with me at the Raceway until eleven—but so had Ward and Wanda, at least most of the time. Harry Ward had been dancing at the Plaza until two in the morning, and his mother had been at the opera and home by eleven herself. It had to be DeLillo. But somehow that didn't feel right. Something was percolating in the back of my head. But what?

The tuna was sitting where I'd left it on the counter by the telephone. I put some mayonnaise into the can along with what was left of the fish and stirred it all around. Then I started thinking about Cissy Holder. When the tuna and the mayo were all nice and mixed, I dumped the whole mess in the garbage and went into the living room.

I hadn't been home much in the last week, but the place looked like it always did. Dull. A living room with a lot of furniture that always seemed to start sagging just when we had finished paying for it. The dining room table Bea and I had gotten when we were married, jammed into the corner of the living room next to the kitchen door. A hall with a bedroom halfway down and a bathroom at the end. Every apartment I've ever lived in has been set up like that. Funny how they always assume that the toilet should be your final destination.

During the afternoon, somebody had slipped a bulletin from the Building Association under the door. Another meeting this Thursday to talk about rent strikes. Vandalism on the second floor. Registration time for the Jewish Community Center Summer Camp for Senior Citizens. Special buses to take you to six different kinds of churches Easter Sunday.

I took off my jacket and remembered the card from Gary, Rowena's kid. Suddenly skiing didn't seem stupid any more. Right now, Colorado sounded like a nice place to be. Clean, and lots of steep hills you could really get moving on. For a year now Rowena has been bugging me to move out there. Harry could use some help in the business, she always tells me, and you know how much the kids love you. I've been waiting to hear it from Harry himself how much he wants his brother-in-law as a partner.

I was just thinking how tired I must be to even consider leaving the city, when the phone rang. I dropped the postcard on the coffee table and went back to the kitchen.

At first I couldn't hear a thing. Just some brushing and sighing, like a record of Twilight in the Forest.

"Who's there?" I demanded.

The sighs rose to a whisper. "It's Peter Hecht, Mr. Jacoby. I have to keep my voice low or my parents will hear."

Peter Hecht. About time he surfaced. I sent Colorado back where it belonged and sat down on the kitchen stool to hear what he had to say. But all I got was the brushing noises, even lower than before.

"You'll have to speak up if you expect me to hear you," I shouted.

"Just a minute," he whispered. There was some

shuffling and a few soft thuds, then Hecht's normal voice. "Is that better?" he asked.

"Of course it's better. Where are you?"

"In the linen closet. The cord just stretches under the door, and I thought the towels would act as soundproofing." His voice started to quaver. "Mr. Jacoby, I had to call. What can we do?"

I pictured him crouching there in the closet, stuffed around with sheets and towels. At least he didn't want to talk about what we hadn't done. Like find Cissy Holder before she was killed.

"I didn't kill her, Mr. Jacoby," he said tremulously. "But I don't know who did. I had to take my mother to the dentist at lunchtime, but I got back to Mount Vernon by one-thirty. I didn't see anybody go in or out all day."

Not even me.

"I feel terrible," Peter added. "Maybe I could have saved her."

I tried to comfort him.

"Don't worry, kid. By then Cissy Holder had been dead for almost two days. She was murdered Tuesday night."

Some consolation.

"So they know that now." He said it as though he still wasn't convinced. "I can't really believe she's dead," he confessed.

"Well, she is, Peter, and you and I are going to find out who did it." He was going to have to face it sooner or later. And besides, I needed him.

"Do the police have anyone watching your house?" I asked.

"I don't think so," he answered after a few seconds. "They released me into my father's custody. But I have to tell you, Mr. Jacoby . . . I wasn't completely honest with you before. Last year, Cissy and I got a little more involved than I told you. And then I did some pretty crazy things."

It was a good thing Abe Minelli had filled me in. The kid would have been tucked in with the towels all night at the rate he was talking.

"Let's forget about last year," I suggested. "I know all about it. The big questions for now are, do you still have that car and can you get out of the house?"

"Well, I don't know." He seemed confused. "That is, yes, I have the car, but no, I don't see how I could get out. For one thing, my parents would be really furious if I left without telling them, but they'd never let me go if I asked. And anyway," he added belligerently, "I don't want to go anywhere. Cissy's dead, so what's the point?"

"Don't you want to find out who killed her? Come on, Peter. You got me into this. It's too late to start getting shy now."

One thing you learn to do as an officer is to bully people, especially in a good cause. It's amazing how many witnesses and even victims get cold feet in the middle of a case. Or maybe they just get tired of it all. Whatever it is, you gotta keep them with you or else all your time gets thrown away. I worked on Hecht for another few minutes, and finally I brought him around.

"What do you want me to do?" he asked reluctantly.

"Right now, I want you to go to sleep. It's too dark to do anything, anyway. But as soon as it begins to think about getting light, say around five-thirty, I want you to rise and shine and come pick me up. Better yet, make that five sharp you get up. We ought to be back in Larchmont by six. And Peter," I added, "since you'll be leaving so early and all, I don't think you have to wake your parents or tell them where you're going." The last thing I wanted was a furious father descending on my door.

Chapter 36

By the time I hung up, it was getting on to one-thirty in the morning. It wasn't worth the trouble of getting undressed for three and a half hours of sleep, so I made myself a big pot of coffee and counted on adrenaline to get me through. One thing I noticed after I turned fifty was that sleep didn't seem as important as it used to—maybe because I could feel the big Sandman starting to breathe down my neck for real.

The Late Late Show was Jimmy Cagney in *White Heat*, which I'd seen three or four times. I watched it anyway. I liked the part where he goes crazy in the prison dining hall, after he finds out his ma's dead. I wondered if prisons were still like that—talking to visitors through the grill, sitting at long tables where you eat with a spoon, tapping out messages through the wall. Maybe somebody I knew would be finding out soon. But who?

Everything seemed to point to Val DeLillo, or at least to somebody acting for him. Cissy Holder had been working for Wanda, and DeLillo wanted to scare his sister out of the business. From what I'd heard, a little murder was just his game. Probably those other girls had worked for Wanda, too. They'd all known Ward, Abe said, and that was where Wanda was finding a lot of her talent. And that would explain why there weren't more stories about how the victim had been a cheerleader and a saint. It would also explain why all of a sudden Wanda was so hot to ditch her fillies and get out of town.

What it didn't explain was the threatening letters she and Ward had been getting. They just didn't fit. That was why I had to go to Larchmont again, to see Ward and to take a look at that boathouse. Abe's men were out there, but I could get around them somehow. Maybe if I were on the spot the whole thing would make more sense.

Three-thirty. Nobody awake but me and the lushrollers, working the drunks sprawled dead in the outbound cars. The back of my head was starting to throb again, and I was beginning to get punchy. As I dozed off, I kept on seeing this figure bending over a table, methodically pasting little pieces of paper to a sheet of cheap yellow stationery. I kept trying to get around the table so I could see the person's face, but things always got in my way. Finally I stumbled and fell asleep.

The next time I woke, Cagney was just about to blow himself up, screaming that the cops would never get him, that he was on top of the world.

I turned off the set and sat there in the dark, alone with my annoying dream. Then all at once the figure at the table started to acquire a face. I was suddenly awake again. I checked the clock. Still too early. All that was left now was to wait for morning. I turned the TV on again to make the time pass.

After the movie was over, there was the sermonette, and then the national anthem, and then nothing. I watched them all. At five o'clock I made myself another pot of coffee and a plate of eggs, and at five-twenty-five I was downstairs waiting by the curb.

At a quarter to six the white Chevy pulled up with Peter Hecht at the wheel, and I saw right away my plans were shot to hell. Abe Minelli was with him.

Abe looked terrible. Wrinkled clothes, wrinkled face, greasy streak down the middle of his head where he kept on fooling with his hair. I only hoped being up all night hadn't taken as much out of me as it had out of him.

I walked over to the car as he rolled down the window.

"What are you doing here?" I growled.

"That's my question," he snapped back. "You don't have to answer, of course," he continued more calmly. "And I warn you that anything you say may be held against you. But I sure would like to know what's going on in what's left of that head of yours."

"You don't have to read me my rights," I said,

climbing into the back seat. "I know them by heart. English and Spanish. But since *friendship* and *trust* are thicker than water, I'd be happy to tell you all."

"Cut the sarcasm crap," Abe ordered. "I've been up all night with a hysterical woman, and I've had about all the innuendos I can handle."

"Something the matter with Alice?" I asked, suddenly frightened.

"Alice is fine. Or she was the last time I saw her, which was too damn long ago. I was nuts to take on this job at my age." Abe really was at the end of his rope. "Nah," he said disgustedly, "the lady in question is Mrs. Helen Ward, and let me tell you, when that type blows her cool, she really blows it." Abe turned to Peter Hecht. "Go take a walk, kid. Me and Mr. Jacoby have some talking to do."

When Hecht was fifteen feet down the sidewalk, Abe turned back to me.

"Lieutenant Rodriguez was out in Larchmont questioning her husband about his treatment of these three victims when she started in. First it was just little digging remarks, interrupting the questioning. But then she started dropping little hints about her husband's affairs. It looks like Ward may have been more involved with these girls than we thought. At least that's what his wife says. Her theory is that he seduces them and then murders them when he gets bored. She wanted Rodriguez to arrest him on the spot. She even called in her son as a witness that the old man was an s.o.b. who beats her up all the time. Then she got violent, and Rodriguez had to radio the village police for help. I went over myself to check it out when I heard." Abe sat there shaking his head at the memory.

"And then," he complained, "just when we got Mrs. Ward sedated and it looked like I was going to get a chance to go home, who pulls up next to us at the first red light but this character." He tilted his head in Peter's direction. "A murder suspect out for a spin on the Post Road at 5 A.M. He looked so guilty, I had to pull him over."

"And he, of course, had to tell you right away where he was heading," I added.

As if he knew we were talking about him, the kid turned around to face me for the first time. I saw what Abe meant about looking guilty. I turned around before he could come over to apologize.

"Well, Inspector Minelli," I said in my best police academy voice, "I'm afraid we're going to have to renew your beat assignment. In other words," I explained, "back to Larchmont. I've finally got a handle on this thing."

Abe shook his head. "No way, Quent. I came out here to tell you I can stretch the rules just so far. I don't like to treat you like a suspect, and you know it, but I can't have you messing up my investigation, either. Especially not when I'm working outside my district. You're the one who went for early retirement. So start retiring."

"Not now," I protested. "I'm on to something, I know it." Abe just raised his hands in a gesture of helplessness. I decided to go for broke and took out the envelope Ward had given me.

"See this?" I asked. Abe turned around briefly, then settled back to staring over the dashboard.

"Sure, I see it. And I even know what it is. Whadda you think I've been doing all night—baying at the moon? Bronovitch cracked as soon as I started talking to her. It's one of those letters she's been getting."

"Wrong," I said triumphantly. "It's one of those letters Eli Ward has been getting. With all the hubbub over there last night, maybe he didn't get around to telling you about them. But I think you'll be interested in this one—he says he found it in his boathouse, pinned to a bloodstained dress, the day after Cissy Holder was killed. If you go out to Ward's house, I think you'll find the dress. Maybe in the garbage. Maybe in the library safe. But somewhere out there you'll find it."

Abe was ready to leave right away. He pulled out his radio, but I leaned over the seat back and held his arm.

"I scratched your back, Abe. Now you scratch mine. The kid and I are coming along."

Abe grimaced, then nodded. He motioned Peter Hecht to get back in the car. We were off.

Chapter 37

The ride north on the New England Thruway was quiet. From the personal attention Abe was giving the case, it was clear he thought it was part of something bigger—at least the murders last week, and maybe even the string of killings last Christmas. On the news, they were already starting to talk again about the Santa Claus Slayer. There'd never been any real progress on those cases, and the homicide boys were starting to look bad. Looking bad is not something Abe Minelli likes to do. If he could close those files that would make up for a lot of grief.

Right now, though, Abe didn't even have enough evidence to bring anybody but Hecht in on suspicion. That was why he had leaped at the note, and that was what he was hoping to find at the doctor's house. Evidence. Even if I never did make detective, I could guess how Abe was operating. In the dark.

But I was a civilian now, and Abe wasn't

sharing any theories. He just stared out the window. It was the kid who finally broke the silence.

He'd been so quiet, I'd amost forgotten him. But while I'd been trying to guess what was on Abe's mind he'd been looking at it from his own angle, like everybody does.

"You know, Mr. Jacoby," he said, "I'm supposed to go back to school on Monday. I mean, Cissy Holder is dead, and in two days I'm supposed to go back to studying physics and American literature and Latin. Does that seem as queer to you as it does to me?"

Abe shot him a look, then went back to surveying the landscape. If Peter Hecht was having trouble believing that his girl was dead, he couldn't even begin to understand that some people considered he might have killed her. I mumbled something about life being funny, and thought about what Abe had told me about the kid's behavior last year. What would he be like when the reality finally sank in? Would he go off the handle again? That reminded me of Mrs. Ward. If Abe wouldn't talk about the case, maybe he'd at least talk about her.

He was more than willing. The turn off the Thruway onto the local streets seemed to have revived him, and he started to gab, just like the old days when we were both working the Lenox Avenue line up in Harlem.

"It was wild, Quent. Absolutely wild. I've

never seen anything like it. Of course, Mrs. Ward was pretty far gone by the time I got there, but still, the strength of that woman was just unbelievable." He glanced at Peter, then decided to ignore him. "Two officers and the son had to hold her down while the doctor shot her full of sedatives," he whispered confidentially.

"Not that the stuff seemed to do much," he continued. "When I arrived she was still jumping all over the place, threatening to scratch the eyes out of anyone who got in her way, screaming about how her husband was the angel of evil and everything he touched turned to death. Funny thing was, the only calm character in the joint was the son. While all this was going on, he kept on apologizing, like he had somehow set her off. Turns out he's used to it—she's left her husband twice already, once just before they moved east from Chicago, and once just before they shipped the kid off to prep school. Both times she went through a stage of hysteria, then collapsed. They'd find her at the hospital. Ward said he could tell she was having trouble, but he hadn't seen how close she was to another total breakdown."

Abe stopped suddenly. The anonymous letters must have clicked in his mind the same way the story he was telling clicked in mine. These murders had looked all along more like the work of a psycho than a pro. The features on the figure at the table were getting clearer.

I remembered what Ward had said in the hospital about how his handsome wife Helen was falling part. I hadn't figured at the time he meant it literally. But was her frenzy strong enough to drive her to murder? Dollars to donuts, Abe was wondering the same thing. I could bet he'd hate like hell having to give up a biggie like Val DeLillo as his prime suspect. But he might have a few more surprises before the day was over.

"We're here," Peter said in a cracking voice. He sounded shaken by Abe's story. I wondered if he could take what was coming.

Chapter 38

Overnight, all the forsythia buds had decided to open. It was hard to believe so much sorrow coming to such a cheerful-looking house— until you noticed the police car parked crosswise to block both sides of the garage. As we were coming up the walk, a husky fellow in shirt-sleeves stepped out the front door. I recognized him as one of the detectives from the hospital lot last night. He stopped himself in mid-yawn and snapped to attention when he saw us.

"All quiet right now, sir," he reported. "Mrs. Ward is asleep. The doctor is down by the water. Guess you can't blame him for needing some fresh air."

Abe just nodded quickly and veered around the flagpole. He was hot on the trail and no mistake. When we got to the water, though, it was a typical case of hurry up and wait. The boathouse was locked and the place was deserted. A blue dinghy was tied to a red and white mooring about twenty yards out from the dock. Further out we could see a lone sailboat, too far away to tell who was in it.

Abe let out a curse and ran to the end of the dock, waving his arms like a semaphore. The sailboat was scooting through the water. Just when Abe got to the end of the dock, the boat snapped around and shot off in the other direction. It was impossible to tell if there was any connection.

Abe sighed resignedly and sat down on the wooden ramp that led from the dock to the boathouse.

"That's what being a detective is, Quent," he announced disgustedly. "Nothing but wasted time and indigestion." He peeled a Tums from the roll in his pocket and munched reflectively.

I was punchy from fatigue and nerves, ready to talk about anything. "You ever been out in one of those jobs?" I asked, pointing toward the water.

"You kidding?"

"Me neither," I admitted. "I still got a shirt Bea gave me when I got out of the army, though. One of those tropical numbers, tan with green palm trees and red sailboats. I always used to tell her I'd get around to wearing it when some millionaire asked me out on his yacht."

Peter Hecht was standing behind us. "He seems to be coming in now," he said quietly. "See how he's tacking to approach the mooring?"

"You a sailor, too, kid?" Abe asked sharply.

"Not really," he answered defensively. "Not like Dr. Ward. Only a couple of summers at camp. But I can tell when somebody is coming in."

Indeed he could. At first I thought it might be Harry in the boat, but now that he was closer I could see it was Eli Ward, wearing a yellow slicker with the hood pulled up. It must have been cold out there, this early in the morning. The sun was just beginning to warm the wood of the ramp. I stood up, wishing I had worn warmer pants.

Ward must have seen us by then, but he just went about his business, pulling down the sail and wrapping everything up in orange tarpaulin. When he was all through, he stepped into the rowboat, untied it, and rowed it to the dock. Only after he had taken the oars out of the boat did he nod a kind of greeting. He didn't seem any too happy to see us.

Abe didn't waste any more time. He had sent an officer out last night for a routine questioning of someone who had known the victim, but now he smelled something bigger. Much bigger.

"I hear you've got a nice little racket going with Val DeLillo," he said for openers. "Is it part of the deal that you let him use your setup here to get rid of his bodies?"

Ward glared at me, but I shook my head helplessly. He was crazy if he thought he was going to hold on to any of his secrets now, but I hadn't told Abe anything and I wasn't about to start. I wouldn't have to.

Ward didn't know Abe like I did, though. He tried to tough it out.

"I don't know what you are talking about, Inspector Minelli," he said firmly. "Your man came here very late last night and insisted on talking to me about Cissy Holder: a very sad case, but one I know next to nothing about. And in talking to your officer, I precipitated a partial breakdown in my wife's health, a breakdown to which I regret to say you were a witness. I would have thought I had already given enough to your investigation, but now you seem to be accusing me of something else—I don't even know what. I think I deserve at least an explanation."

Abe was all patience. "Sure, I'll explain," he said kindly. "Five young women, all either temporary or permanent residence of the city of Mount Vernon, have been killed in the last four months. In each case, the body of the victim was badly mutilated. In each case, we don't know who did it. By a strange coincidence, each of these young women had at one time or another come to you for some form of counseling."

Ward started to interrupt. "Yes, I know," Abe added. "I know you see hundreds of young people every month. Still, it's what you might call an interesting coincidence. Now, four of these victims were abandoned on the street, their bodies neatly packed in plastic garbage bags. But the fifth, Miss Cissy Holder, she washed up on the other side of the Sound, and she didn't get there on her own. I'd like to look over your boat and your dock, Dr. Ward. That is, if you can spare the time."

Ward grabbed the chance. "As a matter of fact, I can't spare the time. As you saw, Inspector Minelli, my wife is not a well woman. I'm sorry you were a witness to it all, but I hope under the circumstances you will understand why I can't talk to you now."

He turned around, like he expected us to have vanished already. That kind of stuff might work with his medical students, but it didn't cut much mustard with Abe.

"But you had time to go out sailing," he noted. "I kind of thought you and your wife would be on your way to the hospital by now."

"Helen is asleep inside," Ward answered grudgingly. "Our son is with her. When she begins to wake he'll call me. I've already made arrangements for her treatment."

"That's okay," Abe conceded. "I thought for a minute you were maybe planning to take her out for a boat ride."

Ward glanced out at the mooring, surprised. "I rarely sail myself this early in the season. Too much danger of storms for a boat that size. I wouldn't have it in the water at all, but my son had some notion about how he would do it now rather than wait until June. Very wise of him. He must have seen this warm weather coming." Ward clenched his fist, as if he was mad at himself for even talking to Abe. "I might add," he said more coldly, "that I do not now and never have used my boat for illicit purposes. If I understand you, Inspector Minelli, these are serious accusations you're making. If you persist, I'll have to call my lawyer."

"Yeah," Abe agreed. "You better do that. But first I want to see your boat. And also that dress, the one that came with the note on it. And don't worry about technicalities," he added. "I just happened to bring along a search warrant."

Chapter 39

There was a long silence. I could hear all kinds of noises I hadn't noticed before. Somewhere out on the water a bell was clanging. Next door, someone was starting up a car. I could almost hear the wheels whirring in Ward's head.

"Yes," he sighed at last. "I suppose you should see it. But remember that my wife is a very sick woman. Try not to disturb her."

As if on signal, we heard an enormous racket and screams coming from the house. It sounded like no human noise I'd ever heard. Dr. Ward's expression turned to panic. "Helen!" he cried.

That was all he said, but we all caught the tension right off. The next minute the four of us were charging up the lawn, Ward leading. He almost tore the handle off the door to that back sun room. I figured Abe hadn't been exaggerating—the wife must be a honey when she got going.

The sun room was pretty much intact, but the living room looked like the original model for the day after the night before. The drapes had been torn off the front windows and the rods left dangling from the walls. There were sofa cushions everywhere, and somebody had thrown a full ashtray against the wall. There was more, but I didn't have time to take it all in. Ward hadn't even broken stride, and we all followed him out of the living room, through the front hall, around to the dining room, and through the swinging door into the kitchen. That was where the noise was coming from, and that was where the action was.

At first it was just a wail and a lot of banging, but as we got into the dining room you could make out the words.

"They can't have him." *Crash.* "They can't have him." *Crash.* "They can't have him." *Crash.*

Ward was the first into the kitchen, then Abe, then the other officer, then me. Peter Hecht didn't seem too sure he wanted to follow, but finally he piled in too. It was a big kitchen, but we were a crowd.

And there was Mrs. Ward. Her mouth was smeared with the remains of yesterday's lipstick and her skirt was pulled all out of line. But what you really noticed was her eyes. I don't think she even saw us. She looked staring-blind, like the animals sometimes do when they've been in the zoo too long.

There really wasn't much we could do. She was backed into a narrow space between the wall and the refrigerator, with both hands around the handle of a big, nasty-looking butcher knife. The only thing she could reach was the refrigerator, and the knife blade just skittered off the metal. That explained the clanging. It was terrifying the way she went after that machine with the knife, like she wanted to cut out its heart.

Ward had his bag out and was getting a needle ready, but there was no way he or anyone else was going to get near enough to give it to her and come out alive. Then Harry Ward stepped forward. He'd been standing just out of his mother's reach. I guess he was the one who'd cornered her. Or maybe he'd just coaxed her there. He didn't look like he'd been in any kind of a struggle. His hair was as perfectly combed as ever. But he looked tired. Very tired.

"It's all right, Mother," he said. It was more a plea than a statement of fact. "It's all right," he repeated. "I'll take care of you. I'll take care of everything. You know I always do when it gets too bad. Don't worry. It's going to be all right."

As he talked, his mother stopped banging. She still held her grip on the knife, but the yelling had sunk to a sob. "They can't. They can't," she blubbered.

"It's all right, Mother," Harry said again. He seemed ready to keep saying it till he dropped. "I'll make it all right. Just give me the knife and I'll take care of everything. I promise. Like I always do," he added more bitterly. "I'll make all the bad parts go away."

When she handed over the knife, there was a

long silence, and then this whooshing noise. I realized we'd all been holding our breath. Her husband was the first to move. This time the sedative took effect right away. Helen Ward looked like a crumpled pile of laundry. She started to snore.

Abe wasn't taking any chances. He took out a set of handcuffs and put them on Mrs. Ward, ready for whenever the sedative wore off. He started toward the phone, then hesitated. He looked at me questioningly. About time we'd become partners again. I nodded and reached over to pull the knife from Harry's fingers before he could get any ideas.

"I tried," Harry said as Abe snapped a second pair of cuffs on the boy's wrist. He wasn't looking at anyone in particular. I guess he was talking to himself. I was afraid he'd have a lot of time for that in the future.

"I tried to stop it . . . to find the letters before anyone else . . . to stay with her at night. But she slipped away, and she killed them, and then I would find her here, just standing by the car . . . and she would always tell me right away what she had done. And where she had left the body. I think she would have told anyone," he added confusedly. "She was happy. She wanted to tell."

He turned to me. "I couldn't just leave them there," he insisted. "I couldn't send my mother to prison. I tried to clean them up, put them where they would be found. I tried to stop her. I tried."

He glared at his father. "You didn't even try to help her," he said.

"Maybe . . ." Ward started, trailing off before he finished the sentence. "A plea of insanity . . . no court would convict her . . ."

"Maybe not," Abe said flatly. "But your son's a big boy now, and he's in this, too. There comes a time," he added gently, "when nobody can make all the bad parts go away."

Abe motioned to Officer Rodriguez, who put his hand on Harry's shoulder. "Come on," he said.

They circled the kitchen table on their way to the door. Harry bent for a moment over the crumpled heap. "Don't worry, Mother," he said for the last time. "It's all right. I don't mind. I'll help you." Who knows? Maybe she heard and felt better. He straightened up and stopped in front of his father, and for a second, I had the idea he was going to spit in the old man's eye. Ward must have thought so, too, because I saw him flinch, but Harry just turned sharp and marched through the swinging door.

Abe was at the kitchen telephone, calling the local police to send their men back with an ambulance. In the next room I could hear the detective reading Harry his rights. With Harry gone and Mrs. Ward knocked out, the kitchen went back to what it was—a big sunny room with starched curtains and lots of counter space, like a feature in some magazine at the check-out lane. Even the knife on the table looked innocent, like it was just waiting around for a nice salami or a loaf of rye. In another few minutes they'd have it tagged and bagged, ready to see if it matched up with the holes in Cissy Holder's body, but they didn't need me around for that.

Between the paste-up notes full of fingerprints and the scene in the kitchen, plus the dress that was around there somewhere, Abe should have no trouble putting the facts behind my 3 A.M. vision. He and Eli Ward still had a lot of talking to do, but I didn't feel like hearing it. I knew Abe would work out some kind of deal to get the goods on Val DeLillo while he was at it, but right now all I was interested in was going home.

Peter Hecht agreed. It had been a rough week for him, I guess, and this morning couldn't have been the lightest part of it. Not that he said so. All he did was ask Abe if he was free to go now.

Abe hung the receiver back on the wall. "Yeah, you can go," he said grudgingly. Abe always did hate to let go of a good suspect. "Nothing official, you understand, but it looks like you're off the hook."

I asked Peter if he could give me a ride home. No telling when the buses ran on Saturday around here. Maybe they didn't run at all when the cleaning women weren't working.

As we were going down the front walk, an ambulance pulled up to the curb.

"Hey, bud," the driver called to me. "This the Ward house?"

I nodded and turned to join Peter at the car, but I was stopped again by a middle-aged man who had walked over from across the street.

"Are Eli and Helen all right?" he asked anxiously.

"Not exactly," I answered. "But they're being taken care of." He wasn't reassured. I left him flipping a rake nervously from hand to hand while he watched them bring a stretcher up the front steps.

Chapter 40

The forsythia were still blooming as we drove back up Pilgrim Point Road and out through town toward the Thruway. Tomorrow was Easter, and all the stores were jammed. The corner deli had put a four-foot Styrofoam Easter Bunny in the window, surrounded by small foil-wrapped chocolate rabbits, right next to the tiered rack that showed off their eight different kinds of bagels.

Hecht was right. It was hard to believe people were still going about their ordinary business, after all we'd been through. But then again, that was the point. The whole reason for finding out who killed Cissy Holder was so that other people could go about their ordinary business, not having to worry if they were going to get knifed any minute.

It took forever, but we finally made it through the local traffic and onto the open road. Abe had started talking when we pulled off the Thruway. Hecht started talking when we pulled on.

"I don't get it," he said hesitantly. "I mean, I just don't understand any of it. Why would Mrs. Ward want to murder Cissy Holder? And those other girls. And why would Harry help her?" He checked the rear-view mirror, then turned to me. "Do you think she was jealous of girls like Cissy?"

"Looks that way."

"But that's crazy," he protested.

I couldn't think of a better word, so I let it ride. We dodged a rented van driven by some maniac who obviously planned to get to California tonight.

"All right," Peter agreed. "So she was jealous. You don't kill somebody because you're jealous."

The kid had a lot to learn. "Helen Ward did," I said. "Or at least I'll be mighty surprised if she didn't." Peter still looked lost, so I explained.

"Cissy Holder was killed some time between seven and eleven Tuesday night. That eliminates you and me and Eli Ward and Wanda."

"Wanda?"

"The landlady. We were all at the Raceway Tuesday night, and a job like that, with a knife and a dump in the water, you can't do in the twenty minutes between races. That still left Val DeLillo, and the Sheik, if he was working for Wanda, and Lord knows who Abe figured might be working for you."

"DeLillo? The Sheik? Who are these people?"

"Just a couple of characters you don't want to know. The thing is, all these leads came from Cissy Holder. What about those three other girls dead in Mount Vernon? All killed the same way, more or less. I knew it had to link up somehow with the Santa Claus Slayer. For a while I thought DeLillo was just trying to get back at his sister, but DeLillo's too good at this kind of thing, and it just didn't make sense to think of these murders as a pro job. All those girls hacked up and dumped around, and then neatly picked up and packed away for the sanitation men—it spelled psycho no matter what way you arranged the letters. The confusing thing was that I hadn't figured the two of them working against each other."

"I still don't understand," he complained.

I tried to explain as best I could. I wasn't sure I understood either.

"Harry Ward and his mother may care about each other a whole lot," I began, "but that doesn't mean they're on the same wavelength. Harry was trying to save his mother, going around picking up the pieces of the mess she'd made. Literally. I guess protecting her seemed more important to him than worrying about anybody else who might die along the way. But Mrs. Ward wanted to be caught. She wanted to make her husband notice. That's why she was sending those letters, and that's why it just got her more frustrated and more violent when Harry intercepted them. He thought he was protecting her, but he was just goading her on."

It was beginning to hit me how tired I was. I looked out at the marshlands that line the highway in the upper Bronx. Another ten years and it will all be landfill and co-ops. Too bad. It's nice to be reminded every once in a while what this place really looks like underneath.

Hecht still had his eye on the road and his mind on this morning. "When we went into the kitchen," he said, "I thought Inspector Minelli was going to arrest only Mrs. Ward."

"So did I. Good thing he realized he was leaving something out."

"What made you know it was Harry as well as his mother?"

"For one thing, the timing. Nobody was unaccounted for long enough to do it all alone. But what really made me see it was you."

"What?"

"Sure. You. Pull over here," I directed, pointing to what actually seemed to be a parking space near my building. He cut the engine, but neither of us got out.

"Remember when you were talking about going back to school on Monday?"

Hecht nodded.

"Well," I said, "that's when I figured it out. Two murders the week after Christmas, two murders the week before Easter. If we were dealing with your ordinary Druid-type nut who listens to the voices that tell him what to do, it would be the same each time—just before the holiday or just after, but not one of each. And if it were Mrs. Ward alone, why the big wait in between? When you started talking about vacation it hit me. Harry Ward came down from school for Thanksgiving, just when Wanda was calling up his father and beginning to get to his mother. Then he was here between Christmas and New Year's. And tomorrow he was going to go back to school just like you, except that Harry goes to school far away, because his mother can't stand to have him around. It struck me as queer right from the beginning, how she always talked about being with her son but then always managed to send him away—off on an errand, out of the room, out of her life. It's not the kid himself, but whatever he represents in her mind. Maybe she never really wanted to have him. Maybe Harry is somehow tied up in her head with Ward's messing around with other women. Or maybe the poor kid just looks like his father did when Helen met him—a living reminder of what she was fool enough to marry. Whatever it is, his being home is what sets her off. Everything he tried to do for her just made it worse."

I gave Hecht a few minutes to digest that, then changed the subject.

"You know," I speculated, "I doubt very much it was just coincidence that Abe Minelli picked you up this morning. After the way you carried on last year, he figured for sure you were his man. Did you really go to her parents' place with a gun?"

The kid blushed. "I was upset," he protested. "And I really don't want to talk about it right now."

Stupid of me. "I'm sorry," I apologized. "Anyway, it's a lucky thing for you we got together, kid. If I hadn't taken you to the Raceway, where would your alibi be?"

Hecht smiled, and I realized it was the first time I'd seen him do it. His front teeth were crooked.

"I guess I would have had an alibi anyway," he said. "If it weren't for you, I would have been where I am almost every Tuesday night. Helping run the recycling center at the Second Methodist Church. My father's the minister."

No wonder he felt a little strange about Uncle Quentin, the racetrack tout.

"So if I hadn't dragged you around all night, you never would have gotten hauled in at all. Look," I offered, "if you want me to talk to your parents or anything . . ."

"That's nice of you," he said. "But I guess they'll understand. Inspector Minelli will probably be talking to them soon, right?"

I nodded, relieved. Conversations with the clergy are not my specialty.

We had rolled down the windows, but the car

was getting like a greenhouse, all hot and steamy from sitting in the sun. Hecht cleared his throat.

"You know, Mr. Jacoby, you're right anyway. I mean, it was a lucky thing we got together. Not for me, maybe, because Cissy's still dead and nothing can change that—I don't want you to think I've forgotten that—and I guess the police would have found Mrs. Ward without us, but I keep thinking about the place Cissy was staying, and the way she was living. I mean, there are lots of other girls like Cissy. The police wouldn't have found that so fast without us, would they?"

"Probably not," I agreed. There were plenty more where Wanda came from, but he could find that out on his own. If he were lucky, he'd never know.

"There's one more thing," Peter said. "I don't want you to think I've forgotten about paying you. I figure I owe you another hundred and fifty dollars, but I haven't exactly been able to get to the bank. I will on Monday, though, for sure. I can bring it over after school if you'll be home."

The kid was trying to be grown up, like he always was, but it made me feel cheap to even think about money. I hadn't gone through with this deal to turn a buck.

"Keep your money, Peter. I won't be home on Monday. I promised a friend I'd go out to Meadowlands with him to watch an exhibition match. He gave up soccer for Lent and wants to get back to his old vices as soon as he can." I wondered if Sam would still be speaking to me when he found out what I'd done to his sister's kid.

"Tell you what," I suggested. "Next time you're passing the track, put something on the Exacta. If you win big we'll split it."

He smiled again. "It's a deal. And thank you for everything, Mr. Jacoby."

"Sure, kid," I said, stepping out. "And take one last word of advice from your Dutch Uncle Quentin."

He looked up expectantly.

"Get rid of this car. It's a gas guzzler. Mass transit is the thinking man's alternative."

Chapter 41

I guess I was kind of expecting to find Sam Fuentes parked outside my door. I know I wasn't surprised.

As soon as he saw me get off the elevator he was up off his heels, leaving Mrs. Munoz's kid to finish off the game of acey-deucy by himself.

"Eh, Jacoby," he wheezed, trotting down the hall toward the elevator. "Where you been? I be lookin' for you since eight o'clock. Here, Maybelle's—all over, man. I even look for you *outside*," he added significantly.

I got ready for whatever load of Latin catastrophe Sam was about to wish on my head. He'd told me about his famous temper often enough, but I've never seen it in action beyond a bout or two with the druggist when Sam thought he was being bilked on his Medicaid. Now was my chance.

Except, as usual, I had figured things just a little bit off. Instead of beating my head in, Sam wanted to thank me.

"Seven this morning," he announced, "before sunrise almost, my niece Immaculata is on the telephone. She just back from the police station, see, with my cousin Rafael, where they both gone for to get out my sister's son, Carlos. That crazy kid, he try to be a big hoodlum, like a king of the Syndicate." The way Sam said it, it sounded like Sin-dee-kay, but I guess I knew what he meant.

The story looked like it was going to be a long one, so I started toward my door. Sam trotted along, jabbering away about how he could hear his sister having hysterics in the background, screaming and carrying on about how her baby was a good boy, never in trouble, and all like that.

When I got the door open Sam pushed past me and made himself at home in the La-Z-Boy recliner. The more excited he gets, the more Sam lapses into Spanish, which I don't follow all that well if he's going fast. Which Sam was. But as far as I could tell, the big thing was that I hadn't pressed charges on the assault business.

"So Carlos, see, he so thankful, he swear to his mama in the name of his father and his grandmother, *mia madre, dama santa* . . ." Sam broke off to cross himself. "He swear he will never again do nothing criminal. *Nada. Jamás.*"

The Sheik's mother may have gotten him to give up his big plans, but I bet Abe Minelli laid the ground for her. He can be pretty blunt with guys like Carlos, guys who haven't done anything much yet, but are thinking about it pretty hard. I used to call him in a lot when I collared kids who looked like they could make it back on the straight. Anyway, Sam's family was treating it like the kid's second communion, and apparently I was the one who had led Carlos Washington back to the faith by not pressing charges.

"I tell you, Jacoby," Sam wheezed at me, "next July we have a big family fiesta, we make you honorary cousin. *Primo* Jacoby. You meet all my sweet nieces, and if it's hot I present you my special sno-cone. No water, frozen rum. Is beautiful!"

Sam was settling back to tell me again what a great *hombre* I was to protect his family from such disgrace. I was saved from having to listen to it by the telephone ringing in the kitchen. As I went to answer it, Sam switched on the television to watch the Mets game. In another minute he'd have his shoes off.

It was Abe calling to keep me posted—or, I should say, it was one of the detectives from Abe's office. A girl, yet. Minelli was on another line. While I waited, Officer Jamison filled me in. They'd found the dress all right, and Mrs. Holder had already identified it as Cissy's. The Ward kid was refusing to talk, even to his father's lawyer, but his prints matched the ones on the plastic bags they'd found the other bodies in. His mother's were all over the bodies, and on the letters. There'd always been lots of evidence in those cases, just nobody to attach it to. As soon as they fingerprinted the two of them, the lab went wild.

Mrs. Ward was in Scarsdale Hospital, in the psychiatric ward, and it would probably be a good long time before she got out. Wanda was still being held from last night—with statements from Ward and the Sheik, she could be prosecuted for performing abortions without a license. Abe was still playing games with Ward and his lawyer, making deals to get the doctor to turn state's evidence against both Wanda and DeLillo in return for a shorter sentence for himself.

While Jamison was telling me all this, I was thinking about Eli Ward. Last week he had everything, and today he had less than nothing. His son was on the hot seat as an accessory to murder, his wife was in the cuckoo's nest, and he was on the way to jail himself. His career was over, and even his precious boat was being seized as evidence. If he made a deal with Abe, though, his sentence probably wouldn't be long. When he got out he'd become either a religious fanatic or a methadone junkie, I supposed. Or both. maybe he'd even get his license back—a second chance to do all those good works he was always talking about.

"Mr. Jacoby? Mr. Jacoby, are you still there?"

"Sorry, Jamison. Just a little groggy. I haven't been to bed since the night before last."

"Me neither," she said cheerfully. "Anyway,

Inspector Minelli is free now and wants to talk to you. Can you hold the line?''

I could and I did, and in a minute I was talking to Abe. It was nice to hear someone who sounded as beat as I did. There's nothing like the resilience of youth to set a man's teeth on edge. Abe had just worked out some elaborate way of catching DeLillo doping the horses without having Ward appear on the stand, and he was feeling pretty good about it. When you finally catch somebody like DeLillo, you like to fry his ass good without having to worry about reprisals. I let him tell me again everything Jamison had said a minute before. Then I realized he was asking me a question.

"So how about it, Quent?"

"How about what?" I asked sleepily.

"Jesus, haven't you been listening at all?" Abe snorted. "I just offered you a slot with the Mount Vernon PD and you're already falling asleep on the job. Of course you'll have to take the Civil Service exam and all, but I don't think there'll be any problem.''

"Job?" I repeated. I thought about another week like this one and shook my head. Then I realized Abe couldn't see me.

"You must be kidding," I said. "After this week, all I want is to sleep late and spend the afternoon playing checkers in the sun with the other old geezers. Thanks, Abe, but no thanks.''

I hung up before he could try to persuade me.

I reached into the refrigerator for a bottle of beer, then made it two. Sure enough, when I went back to the living room Sam was still there, stretched out in full recline and flipping through an old issue of *Penthouse* while he watched the game.

"Ah," he grunted, taking a long swig from the bottle I handed him. "Where you been all morning? You miss the big show—that hot Mrs. Rothbender was out sunbathing." He reached out and waved his cupped hands to demonstrate what I had missed, then clucked his tongue sympathetically, mourning my loss. "Hey," he exclaimed, like it was a new idea. "That Mrs. Rothbender, she look just like this blonde used to be crazy 'bout me. She had legs like a jack-hammer, baby, and did she love the way I ran her machine. Rat-a-tat-tat! I ever tell you 'bout her?"

I took a pull at my beer and settled in to hear all about it.

About the Author

J.C.S. Smith is a pseudonym for a noted writer of nonfiction and former resident of New York City.

JOIN THE *SIGNET MYSTERY* READERS' PANEL

Help us bring you more of the books you like by filling out this survey and mailing it in today.

1. Book Title: _____

2. Using the scale below, how would you rate this book on the following features? Please write in one number from 0-10 in the spaces provided.

POOR	NOT SO GOOD		O.K.		GOOD		EXCEL-LENT
0	1	2	3	4	5	6	7	8	9	10

RATING

Overall opinion of book .... _____
Scene on Front Cover .... _____

3. What are your two favorite magazines?
   A. _____
   B. _____

4. Do you belong to a *mystery* book club?
   (   ) Yes   (   ) No

5. About how many mystery paperbacks do you buy each month? _____

6. What is your education?
   (   ) High School (or less) (   ) 4 yrs. college
   (   ) 2 yrs. college   (   ) Post Graduate

7. Age _____   8. Sex: (   ) Male (   ) Female

9. Occupation: _____

Please Print Name:_____

Address:_____

City: _____ State: _____ Zip: _____

Phone #: (   )_____

Thank you. Please send to New American Library, Research Dept., 1633 Broadway, New York, NY 10019.